*Some advice from
Carly Carrothers:*

Beware of single dads! You are bound to get your heart broken if you fall in love with a confirmed bachelor and his adorable kid. I recommend the following mantra, to be said each night before bedtime:

> You don't want to marry the Big Bad Dad.
>
> You don't want to marry the Big Bad Dad.
>
> You don't want to marry the Big Bad Dad.

Of course, that hasn't stopped me from pining away for sexy single dad Mackenzie James—my irresistible new boss. Okay, so I shouldn't be kissing him over coffee each morning, or working late every night. And so what if I help out with the kid now and then? Doesn't mean I'm hoping to marry the guy. Does it?

Well, anyway, try the mantra. Maybe it will work better for you....

Dear Reader,

I love my house. I realize that's an odd thing to say to start off a letter about romances, but…well, it's true. And it's also relevant. The minute I saw my house for the first time, I knew I had to have it. Luckily, I got it—and twelve and a half years later, I'm still happy there. Eden Wells, heroine of Lynda Simons' *The Wedding and the Little White Lie*, felt much the same when she first saw the big old mansion that was up for grabs in a local contest. And being married would make winning so much more likely. So she hooked up with fellow contestant Steve Cooper and…well, let's just say that I think Steve's the *real* prize. Read the book and you'll know just what I'm talking about.

And next up…*Big Bad Dad*, the latest from Yours Truly phenomenon Christie Ridgway. How *does* she keep coming up with winner after winner? I don't know, and so long as she keeps on doing it, I don't care! For Carly Carrothers, there's one cardinal rule in life: Never—but *never*—fall in love with a single dad. Especially when he's your boss. Especially when he's adamantly antimarriage. Especially—oh, forget it! She's hooked. And you will be, too, from the moment you read page one.

And don't forget: After you enjoy both of this month's books, come back again next month for two more great novels all about meeting—and marrying!—Mr. Right.

Yours,

Leslie J. Wainger

Leslie J. Wainger
Executive Senior Editor

Please address questions and book requests to:
Silhouette Reader Service
U.S.: 3010 Walden Ave., P.O. Box 1325, Buffalo, NY 14269
Canadian: P.O. Box 609, Fort Erie, Ont. L2A 5X3

CHRISTIE RIDGWAY

Big Bad Dad

SILHOUETTE YOURS TRULY™

Published by Silhouette Books
America's Publisher of Contemporary Romance

For "my" little girls, my nieces
(in order of appearance):
Sarah, Jenna and Kalley.

SILHOUETTE BOOKS

ISBN 0-373-52073-5

BIG BAD DAD

Copyright © 1998 by Christie Ridgway

This edition published by arrangement with Harlequin Books S.A.

® and TM are trademarks of Harlequin Books S.A., used under license.
Trademarks indicated with ® are registered in the United States Patent
and Trademark Office, the Canadian Trade Marks Office and in other
countries.

Printed in U.S.A.

From the author

Dear Reader,

Most of us have learned to expect the unexpected
in life. But Carly Carrothers, the heroine of
Big Bad Dad, is still capable of being surprised. Just
when she's planning to give her old boss two weeks'
notice, she meets her new boss, sexy Mackenzie
James, who introduces her to his daughter, father,
three dogs, cat and missing snake! How can she say
no when he begs her to stay on the job another
month? I hope you enjoy reading about the other
surprises life has in store for Mack and Carly.

My own life as a wife and mother is full of
opportunity for surprise and the unexpected. The
dishwasher breaks the day of a big dinner party.
The washing machine won't run just as the laundry
pile reaches shoulder height. A doctor's
appointment at 10:00 a.m. and at 9:55 the car
refuses to start. Frustrate me? Yes. Surprise me? No.

Lucky for me, my husband is a whiz at repairs and
at keeping me happy, too. We are raising our two
sons in Southern California, where I enjoy the
sunshine, volunteering at my boys' school, and,
most especially, writing stories about love and its
power to make us all heroines and heroes.

I'd love to hear from you. You may write to me at
P.O. Box 3083, La Mesa, CA 91944.

All the best,

Christie Ridgway

Books by Christie Ridgway

Silhouette Yours Truly

The Wedding Date
Follow That Groom!
Have Baby, Will Marry
Ready, Set…Baby!
Big Bad Dad

1

Carly Carrothers practiced her speech as she turned her sporty sedan into the parking lot of the three-story building that housed Cycle Software on the top floor. "I'm going back to Spenser, Indiana, to marry the new minister.

"I don't have to say that," she reminded herself. She swerved around a crane and a stack of steel beams, then passed a long line of construction-type pickups. Why they were adding another three stories to the building, she had no idea. It certainly wouldn't make the black-glass-and-chrome rectangle any more interesting. There were hundreds of office buildings just like this one throughout Southern California.

Her favorite parking spot, shaded by a spindly date palm, was open. Inside the building, the elevator carried her quickly to the third floor. Okay, okay, she should have taken the stairs, but she wanted to get the speech over with as soon as possible.

The elevator doors parted with a "Star Trek" *whoosh*. Lisa, the Cycle Software office manager, was ensconced at the receptionist's desk. Carly met her familiar, friendly gaze. "Darla must not be in yet," Carly guessed. "What about John?"

At Lisa's head shake, Carly dropped into one of the reception area's tweed chairs. "Darn. Well, let me try it out on you, then." She took a breath. "I'm quitting."

Lisa's eyes widened and her mouth opened.

Carly held up a hand. "Don't say anything yet, let me finish." She'd worked as assistant to the CEO of Cycle Software for five years, and telling John Hart she was leaving the company wouldn't be easy. Another long inhale. "John, I won't go into my personal reasons, I just think it's best that I leave Cycle."

She looked at Lisa anxiously. "You think John will want to know my personal reasons?"

"It's your bad experience with Peter, isn't it?"

Carly ignored the question, contemplating instead Lisa's beach-baby tan and streaked hair. She sighed. "I should have realized years ago I don't belong in California." She touched her own hair, pale blond and curly, contained in a French twist. "This stuff doesn't do well in salt water. And these—" she pointed to her freckles "—don't do well in sunshine."

Lisa didn't seem distracted. "It's about Peter. It's about Peter going back to his ex-wife and daughter."

Carly winced. Losing her relationship with Peter and his daughter, Laurel, had been…a blow. "It's *about* a long weekend spent reflecting upon my life. Anyway, our breakup was months ago."

"But he got remarried on Saturday."

Carly spoke louder. "It's *about* a long phone call with my mother who made me realize what I'm missing back home."

"You've never wanted to go back to Indiana. And hasn't anyone told you? You can't go home again."

Carly spoke louder and slower. "It's *about* men without baggage. No previous marriage. No ex-wife and darling children tugging at their hearts."

"Puh-leez—"

"It's *about* the new Methodist minister in Spenser, Indiana, who my mother says is just perfect for me. Never been married, heart-whole, and looking for a wife."

Lisa shook her head through Carly's entire speech. Kept shaking it.

Carly gave up convincing her friend and looked expectantly down the hall toward John's office. "So when's he coming in?"

Lisa's expression could only be called a smirk. "Oh—in about eight weeks."

"*What?*"

The phone started ringing. Lisa competently answered the call with one touch of a long, manicured nail. "I'm sorry," she said into her headphone receiver. "But Mr. Hart was called out of the country."

Out of the country? John made overseas trips all the time, but he hadn't anything on the calendar for another month.

Lisa continued. "I can refer you to Cycle's new president, however. Mr. Mackenzie James started this morning."

What?

The phone buzzed again, then again, so Carly retreated to her office to click through the E-mail she'd accumulated over the long Memorial Day weekend. Oh, great. Here was one from John, asking that she give the new president, Mackenzie James, her full support.

She'd known Mackenzie was coming, of course, and known she'd be working for him. In a month's time. But as the E-mail explained, John had been called away to Germany thirty days earlier than expected and Mackenzie James had agreed to step in immediately. All during the same weekend that she'd been reevaluating her life over homemade cinnamon rolls—thank you, Mr. Breadman bread maker—chocolate-and-caramel bars and one late-night, almost-teary phone call to her mother.

Her intercom buzzed. She pressed the red button. "Yes?"

"Your new boss is off the phone now," Lisa said through the speaker. "Good luck, Ms. Goodbye Girl."

Carly pushed away from her desk, not allowing herself a moment to reconsider. It would be easier to give notice to a stranger, anyhow. She looked around the familiar clutter of her office as she walked out the door—large window with a view of the busy 405 freeway, dusty-screened computer monitor, corkboard with the smiling school picture of eight-year-old Laurel at center stage. Carly's heart pinched and she grimaced. But she'd leave it all behind—office *and* heartache— in two weeks' time. Maybe less.

Her brief knock on the new president's office door was answered by a pleasant "Come in." Carly took a breath. So far, so good. She pushed it open.

His head bent, Mackenzie James stood behind his desk, flipping through a computer printout. He was wearing the casual dress of a software company exec—

khakis and crisp, white, oxford-cloth shirt. A yellow tie, knotted easily at his throat, bore images of Pinky and the Brain, the lab mice duo of the "Animaniacs" cartoon show.

She loved "Pinky and the Brain" and found herself murmuring Brain's infamous tag line. "Are you pondering what I'm pondering?"

Mackenzie James looked up, a distracted expression on his face.

Carly's already nervous stomach dipped, but before she could get out a more conventional greeting, his phone buzzed.

He picked up the receiver, mouthed at her, "Wait," then half turned as he took the call.

Carly's stomach dipped again at the interruption, but she used the moments to surreptitiously check out the new boss. He was John's age, early thirties, with short-cropped dark hair and crinkly cornered dark eyes. A handsome man by anyone's standards, about six feet tall with an athlete's build.

Carly gripped her fingers together tightly. Handsome didn't mean reasonable, kind or willing to let her go with a minimum of fuss. She watched his strong hands jot down notes as he *hmmed* and *aahed,* and a burn started at the back of her neck. *Nerves.*

The receiver hit the phone cradle with a *clack,* and Mackenzie James looked up again, a polite smile breaking over his face.

Her stomach not only dipped this time, but executed a complete swimmer's turn. Boy, she was anxious. She pasted over the feeling with her own shaky smile. "I'm

Carly Carrothers," she said. "Your—uh—John's assistant."

The phone buzzed again, and he grimaced apologetically and gestured toward the chair in front of his desk as he picked it up. His voice notched a bit lower, and a shiver jogged down Carly's spine. Despite his invitation, she stayed in place behind the chair.

Sheesh. Why so edgy? People quit jobs all the time, she reminded herself. Her gaze slid his way, trying to gauge by his looks how their hello-and-goodbye interview would go.

Then his own roaming gaze found her face. A warm, though impersonal, connection. Her breath caught, but she smiled at him, tentatively, until his eyes narrowed and his gaze sharpened.

For the first time, she realized, he was really looking at her. Seeing her as a person.

Perhaps even as a woman.

Her skin twitched with fur-rubbed-backward discomfort. She couldn't break the eye-to-eye connection, even though her neck burned hotter, and her nervous stomach forced a lump into her throat that wouldn't swallow back into place.

The phone call ended, and she found herself staring at him in silence. She cleared her throat. "Carly Carrothers," she said one more time.

"I'm Mackenzie James. Mack." His voice shivered down her back again. "Glad to meet the one person John guaranteed I can count on."

Ouch.

"We-e-ll." She took a breath, then forced it out as

she cravenly moved her gaze off the man to focus on his pencil cup.

A formless blob of kiddie-clay, it was haphazardly glazed an eggplant purple. His phone started ringing again, and suddenly she didn't want to wait another moment. Not when his eyes made her so jittery. Not when her stomach needed calming and her neck needed cooling. Get it over with, she told herself.

"That's why I'm here," she blurted before he could take the call. "I'm giving my two-weeks' notice."

Mack blinked, and blinked again, then stared, astonished, at the woman across his desk. Had she said two-weeks' notice? He pressed a button and told the receptionist to hold his calls, then focused back on Carly. "You're quitting?"

Just as she opened her mouth, a hammering started on the ceiling right above his head. He couldn't hear a word she said.

Damn construction. And the building management had promised it wouldn't interfere. "Quitting?" he yelled over the noise.

She nodded.

With the yammering hammer echoing inside his skull, he took a brief survey of the contents of his new office. Product specs. Unfamiliar. Program listings. Undecipherable. User documentation. A stack four feet high. An assistant, not much taller, talking about two-weeks' notice. His gaze traveled back to her. *Quitting? Oh, no, you're not.*

He'd learned something from his ex-wife's defection. He wasn't going to let another woman leave him in the second biggest lurch of his life.

As if she could tell their conversation wouldn't be over soon, she finally moved from behind the chair and slid onto its seat. Her legs crossed, then recrossed nervously, causing Mack to focus on the pale, stockinged length of skin that showed below her black skirt.

Nice legs.

She cleared her throat. "I hope my leaving won't be a problem."

That doozy of a comment refocused his attention on the issue at hand. Nice legs or no nice legs, he needed this woman's assistance. Bad.

"Listen, Carly—" He took a moment to soften his voice and strategize. Maybe compliments would work. Hell, they'd better work.

Not that they wouldn't be sincere. John's list of Carly's virtues could start at the third-story window and find its way to the street below. She'd begun as a programmer right out of college, and John had convinced her to abandon bits and bytes to become his assistant a year later.

"John says you have complete knowledge of the product line." Mack tried not to plead. "And the strong points of all the personnel."

Carly executed another leg cross that he sternly ignored. "I've been here five years," she said.

He sighed. She hadn't said, I've completely reconsidered and plan to stay another five.

"And you're great on the job." Mack tried another one of those compliments. According to John, she took up all the slack and then some.

"That's very nice to hear, of course, but..." Her pale legs moved again, drawing Mack around his desk, closer to Carly. Her spine straightened, and she shot him a wary look.

He halted, mentally slapped himself and forced his gaze back onto her face. The skin was pale there, too, with light freckles. The freckle pattern was sporadic and charming, as if his daughter's favorite character, Tinkerbell, had dashed pixie dust across Carly's skin.

She brushed a self-conscious hand over her cheek. "What is it?"

That woke him up. What the hell was the matter with him, anyway? *Contemplating freckles.* Damn. That hammering must've done some damage to his brain.

"What it is is John had to leave, I had to start a new job early, and you're supposed to be helping me." He heard the frustration in his voice. "You've got to reconsider your two-weeks' notice."

She frowned and shifted her legs again. At this closer distance, her movement caused the slightest trace of floral perfume to tease his nose. In Detroit, his assistant had worn a coat and tie and slapped on English Leather every morning.

"Well, actually, I was hoping I wouldn't have to stay the full two weeks. John let the last person who quit leave after a couple of days."

Mack briefly closed his eyes. All the better to think up another argument. All the better to forget about great legs and interesting freckles. "Is it money? Have you had a better offer? I'm certain we could match it...maybe even go a bit higher."

She smiled and shook her head. "It's not about money."

Mack grimaced. "Could we make it about money?"

Carly laughed. "No, no. I've really made up my mind to leave."

"What about guilt? Will guilt work?" Mack smiled at her to soften the edge of the best tool he could think of at the moment.

Carly's own smile died.

Good.

Frown lines appeared between her eyes—clear gray-green eyes, with dark lashes and blond eyebrows—and it suddenly seemed oppressively hot in the office.

Mack reached over and thumbed on the fan that sat atop the six-foot-high oak file cabinet, then leaned against the front of his desk. The air stirred, and so did Carly.

She gripped the arms of her chair and bit her lip. "I know it isn't the best time for me to quit."

The fan turned his way, and a blast of tepid air hit his cheek. "Guilt's working then."

That stricken expression recrossed her face, so he went in for the kill. "Come on. Stay with Cycle. We can talk about more money, different responsibilities."

The fan breezed her way, and her perfume floated by him again. A strand of almost-kinky blond hair escaped from her twist and landed on her lips. Stuck there.

She didn't seem to notice. He couldn't keep his eyes off her mouth and its sheer stain of dark pink color. Another spurt of fan-breeze, another nerve-tingling waft of her perfume.

Maybe it would be better if she left the company, after all. He had a job to do and a household to head and no time to notice a women's perfume or anything else about her.

"Well, you see..."

She seemed hesitant about going on. That strand of blond stayed linked to the corner of her mouth, making his fingers itch. The itching made him think that yes, it would be more prudent to let this valuable, but tempting, Carly Carrothers head off into the world of other employment.

She sighed. "Maybe I should stay for the two weeks."

He groaned inwardly. Not only was she attractive, but she had a conscience, too.

A small, pink-tipped finger came up to hook the strand and pull it free of her mouth.

It should have eased some of his tension.

It didn't.

She drummed her fingertips against her small, square chin. "Shoot. I really wanted to get going on this."

She didn't specify the "this," but relief eased Mack's mind. She would go. Somebody else in the company could bring him up to speed. He started mentally running through the employee roster.

"What about that trip John was supposed to make to San Francisco at the end of June? Who does John have on tap for that?" she asked.

"Me." Maybe one of the junior programmers could work with him. Just for a week or so.

Carly frowned. "You? You don't know anything about the new treadmill program."

Mack nodded. He'd come from a financial software business in Detroit. Cycle's thirty-two employees cre-

ated computer programs designed to regulate and mo-
tivate fitness equipment users. Though begun with exercise bicycles, Cycle currently had products for
treadmills, stair steppers and rowing machines as well.

Carly frowned deeper. "He was going to pitch that
to a brand-new client. Why would he pick you?"

Mack looked out the window and into the safe, anon-
ymous distance. He counted a dozen glass-walled office buildings just like this one. She'd do fine in any
of them, nice, hardworking young woman that she was.
"Because you were supposed to be with me," he said
absently. Maybe the lead programmer would be a better
choice.

"Oh, all right." She sighed. "I'll stay."

"What?" Mack whipped his head around. He'd already imagined her securely ensconced in somebody
else's company. Somebody who didn't like the way her
perfume smelled or the way she smiled or the way the
fan's movement latched that strand of hair to her lips.

It was doing it again, he noticed.

"I've worked here for five years," she said. "I can't
just leave Cycle at a time like this."

What to do? Encourage her to stay because it was
best for the company? Encourage her to go because he
didn't want to be attracted to her?

"Just until the wooing trip's over."

He swallowed. "What?"

"That's what John and I call the visits to potential
clients. Wooing trips. I'll stay until the meeting with
Muscle Machines, Inc. at the end of June and then I'm
outta here."

"Four weeks?" Mack couldn't tell if it was despair or hope in his voice.

She nodded briskly. "Four weeks."

As soon as Carly got back to her office, Lisa sped in and shut the door behind her. "How'd it go?" she asked. Hammering was still going on, as well as other construction sounds, but at a not-so-distracting volume.

Carly grimaced. "I'm staying until the end of the month."

"Four more weeks?" Lisa grinned, then narrowed her gaze. "But what's wrong? Quitter's remorse?"

"I wanted to get out of here sooner," Carly answered. She'd learned by experience the value of quick goodbyes.

"Before somebody else snatches up that minister?"

Carly waved away the concern. "I don't really expect to fall in love with the minister. He's just the symbol of what I'm looking for. What I hope to find back in Spenser."

"A man who's not Peter," Lisa said.

Carly glared at her. "How many times do I have to tell you? It's not *about* Peter. It's *about* finding someone simple and uncomplicated."

"I hate to break it to you, hon, but Forrest Gump is a fictional character."

Carly reheated her glare. "Not someone simple then. Someone without a chip on his shoulder or a load of previous-relationship baggage dragging along behind him."

"Upon entering Spenser a person leaves all chips and baggage at the door?"

Carly sighed. "I give up," she said, pulling a tissue from the box on her desk to wave it at Lisa in surrender. "I'm not going to try to explain anymore."

"Good." Lisa pushed away from the door and flopped into a chair. "Let's talk about the new boss, instead. Is he gorgeous, or what?"

"Lisa, you're married."

"So? That doesn't mean I can only lick my lips over dessert recipes. I still appreciate men." She scooted her chair forward. "I think we should fix him up with someone."

Carly began folding the tissue into a fan. "So he's single?"

"Yep. I asked him."

Ah, the freedoms of married women. Have a single female ask a man that same question, and he'd be dashing straight for the emergency exit.

Lisa drummed her fingers on the arm of the chair. "Who do you think I should set him up with? How about—"

"I don't think he'll have time for a social life," Carly found herself interjecting adamantly. Then she quickly tried covering her gaffe. "At least, not if he plans on getting up to speed in the month I have left here."

Lisa's voice was sly. "What did *you* think of him?"

"He makes me nervous." And her stomach jittery and her neck hot. Weird sensations. "I don't think we hit it off."

"Is that right?"

Carly nodded. "Some people just make each other uncomfortable." So uncomfortable that she wished she could have stuck to her guns and insisted on leaving Cycle right away. But John Hart and Cycle Software had given her job satisfaction and an impressive résumé. The least she could do was ignore her shaky response to Mack.

So what if the man put her on edge? She'd do her job, be here for him, but avoid his company as much as possible.

A knock rumbled on the door. When it opened to reveal the man in question, the rhythm of her pulse leaped to ragtime.

I just don't feel right around him.

"Ah-hah. Just the people I wanted to see," he said.

Carly hoped he meant Lisa.

"I have a favor to ask," he continued, running a hand through the crisp, dark waves of his hair.

Jangling nerves made sitting impossible. Carly rose from her chair and grabbed her water bottle. "Oh, sure," she said valiantly. "Lisa's right here. I'll clear out and go get some water."

"No, no. Don't bother." Mack blocked the door of her office. "I came to find a driver."

Carly kept shuffling forward, hoping he'd move aside. She stopped before her nose bumped against his hard, wide chest.

He looked down at her, bemused. "And since you're already standing, I'll take you."

2

Once in her car, Carly decided the best way to handle her edgy reaction to Mack was to ignore him. She wouldn't be able to do it all the time, certainly, but the trip to his home didn't require her full attention. After absorbing the brief set of directions he gave, she turned on the radio and blanked her mind.

A moment later he reached over with a long arm and thumbed down the volume of the progressive-rock station. "You're probably wondering why I need to go home in the middle of the day."

Of course she was. But when determined to ignore a man, did you pry? "None of my business," she said briskly. "I'll just drop you off and then get back to work." With luck, he'd stay away the rest of the morning and afternoon, leaving nineteen instead of twenty days in his disquieting company.

He shifted restlessly in his seat, stretching his legs as far as they could go in her small car. "Well, uh..." His head cocked in the direction of the speedometer. "It's kind of an emergency. Do you think you could step on it?"

Alarmed, Carly shot him a quick look. "Why didn't

you say so?'' They were on the freeway now, and she steered the car out of the slow lane. "What is it?''

He rubbed his palms over his knees. "Just one more crisis in my full—make that overflowing—life. Corndog's gone." His hands moved from his legs to sift through his hair in obvious exasperation. "Kimmy's screaming like a banshee. The other dogs are going nuts. The cat's slunk into hiding and Dad thinks it might all be a grand assassination plot the cat has hatched to get The President."

Carly gaped. She knew where County Mental Health was, and calculated how many minutes it would take to get there. Or should she drive to the local FBI office? Didn't they handle assassination attempts?

No wonder she'd felt uncomfortable around him. Lunatics could do that to a person.

She shook her head. No. John wouldn't bring a Looney Tune on board. Of course, there was that cartoon tie.... She darted him a look. He appeared normal, okay, downright gorgeous as Lisa said, but—

As if he felt her gaze, his head swiveled toward her and his expression went from distracted to humorous. "You think I'm crazy, don't you?"

Carly swallowed. "The part about the assassination plot made me wonder."

He grinned, going from downright gorgeous to downright devastating. Her pulse rediscovered that Scott Joplin ragtime beat.

"Let me see if I can straighten this out." He held up his fist, then a finger. "Corndog is my half-grown yellow Lab." Another finger left the fist. "Kimmy is my four-year-old daughter. Dad is my father, who lives with us. The dogs are dogs, and the cat is a twenty-pound eunuch who takes his anger out on The President.'' The fully opened hand fell to his thigh, and he sighed like he'd explained everything.

"And The President?" Carly ventured after a minute, when it was clear he thought he was through. "Not, I take it, the one who lives on Pennsylvania Avenue?"

"This exit," Mack directed, then shot her another lethal grin. "Oh, no, The President is a snake."

"An, uh, expression of your political views?" she asked hesitantly.

Mack's grin widened. "He's a small corn snake named for the head of the local vet's association Dad belonged to in Detroit."

Carly smiled back. "That's a relief."

Despite the exchanged smiles, Mack's tension was palpable. "The car's in the shop. My father has a bum knee, but he couldn't leave Kimmy to go chasing after the dog, anyway." He drummed his fingers on his knees, ruffled the map stashed between the seats, then finally began an annoying round of passenger-seat driving as they approached his neighborhood.

"I see the stop sign," Carly said through her teeth, as he opened his mouth for the third warning. She couldn't wait to be rid of him and get back to the office.

They sighed together when she pulled in front of his house. "Thanks," he said, ducking out of the car. Before he had a chance to slam the passenger door, the front door of his two-story white-sided house swung inward and a pink dynamo burst through.

The Energizer bunny? But then the being launched

itself at Mack, and Carly discerned a small girl in the throes of deep distress. "Corndog!" the child wailed.

A gray-haired man, in khakis and a sport shirt, followed more slowly down the front walk, one medium-size and one small dog at his heels. No cat in sight. Carly felt a pang of concern for The President.

Sheesh, she caught herself. I don't even know this snake.

She leaned toward the passenger side and tried pitching her voice over the child's continued cries. "I'll just be going now...." Nothing about this situation concerned her.

Apparently not hearing, Mack turned to place the child on the roof of Carly's car. "Kimmy," he said firmly. "Daddy's here now. Daddy will find Corndog."

All Carly could see of Kimmy was two legs in pink shorts, pink socks topped with lace and dirty, high-top tennies. Typical girl-kid gear. Her heart clenched.

Wound still raw, she noted.

Aware it was really, really time to get going, she opened her door and got out, determined to get Mack's attention over the roof of the car. As she did, a streak of yellow dashed through her line of sight. She pointed a finger down the street. "Is that—"

Mack spun, yelled "Corndog!" and took off in pursuit of the yellow streak, the older man limping at a slower pace behind him. And behind *him* trotted the two other dogs, tongues lolling, teeth gleaming in smiles that bespoke the splendor of a dog's existence.

Carly circled the car to meet the wet brown eyes of the all-in-pink person. She smiled weakly. "Hi."

The little girl blotted her face with her T-shirt, the tears and accompanying runny nose leaving long wet patches on the hem. When Kimmy pushed the shirt back down, a slice of little-kid belly remained exposed.

Carly suppressed an urge to adjust the shirt. *Been there, done that. Got the broken heart.*

All-in-pink took a long, indelicate sniff. "What's your name?"

"Carly. And your dad said you're Kimmy, right?"

Kimmy nodded, her tangle of brown hair swishing around her shoulders. "You have a little girl?"

Carly bit her lip. "No. But I've always liked them."

"You have a dog?"

Carly shook her head.

"Cat? Fish? Snake?"

Carly kept shaking her head. Peter had owned a friendly, fluffy Akita and an entertaining cockatiel. And a daughter, of course.

Kimmy looked off in the direction of Corndog, apparently uninterested in a petless grown-up.

"Would you like to get down?" Carly asked. Then, as soon as Mack or the granddad returned, she could be on her way.

"No," Kimmy said matter-of-factly, and then she shrieked again, "Corndog!" only the sound was happier this time.

Carly turned to catch sight of a strange parade about a block away. At the rear, Kimmy's grandfather, his earlier gait now a Walter Brennan limp that looked like it hurt some. His two dogs pranced and danced at his feet, obviously ready to tug him home with happy teeth if need be.

At the front was the much-slowed yellow streak, presumably the Labrador, Corndog. He looked happy, too, though a man's belt wrapped his collar and connected him to the firm hand of Mack.

Mack.

As if she'd shouted his name, he looked up, and even across the distance of a narrow sidestreet and five lush green lawns she saw his warm eyes, his flashing smile, the almost-summer sun burnishing his dark hair.

Oh, no. As before, her pulse rate shot up.

And as before in his presence, that edgy, uncomfortable, fur-rubbed-wrong feeling surfaced, too, but now she recognized it for exactly what it was.

A precursor to more incautious responses. Because he made her do that, she finally admitted to herself…respond.

He drew closer, and his triumphant grin died. Carly felt his gaze run over her, felt it like eyelashes brushing against her skin, and her insides went tingly, melty. All those treacherous female reactions that didn't give a fig if a man was taken, dangerous or just plain bad for you.

Corndog let out a joyous bark, and she broke her gaze from Mack's to take in the cavalcade of pets, the grandfather, the little girl who sat so cutely on the car. Carly surreptitiously pinched herself. Not that she thought it was a dream, nuh-uh. But because she'd better wake up. Hel-lo, girlfriend. Here's another one.

What the hell was that?

After Carly returned him to Cycle Software, Mack

watched her retreat to her office, forcing his mind off
the female *swish-swish* of her hips.

Nothing, he answered himself. It had better be nothing.

But *something* heated the air between them, had
made the atmosphere in her car markedly...tense. And
the same with the atmosphere in his office, then in her
office, even around the water cooler, anywhere they
happened to find themselves that day and the next
morning, too.

By noon of the second day, Mack figured he was
sending out some celibate-way-too-long vibes that
were making Carly nervous. And if he was going to
get what he needed from her—knowledge of the company—he had to find some comfortable, common
ground with her.

They needed to get acquainted.

So he decided to ask her to lunch. Everybody ate,
didn't they? To the ongoing clatter of hammers and the
screech of saws, he approached her office.

The door was closed, but he'd seen her go inside
just a few minutes before. A knock produced no response, unless a relentless spate of hammer strokes
counted. He raised his hand to knock again—and
nearly rapped her on the nose.

He blinked at the suddenly open door and the vision
of Carly, out of her navy blue skirt and silk shirt and
into a pair of red running shorts and a T-shirt. Her hair
in a frothy ponytail.

"Did you want something?"

Yeah.

But Mack put on his best business smile and said,

"I was going to offer you lunch. Payback for yesterday's ride home." He ran his gaze down her legs to her running shoes. An Air pair. "But I see you have other plans." He wore the same brand of shoes himself.

"Oh," she said with a little shrug, "maybe another time. Though I was happy to help you out."

She didn't look that eager to remember the day before. With a small smile, she brushed past him and he absently trailed her toward the stairway. So much for finding common ground.

Unless... "Wait," he called.

She stiffened, then turned. "Did you want something?"

There was that question again. "I have my running stuff in the car. I was going to stop by the beach on the way home." This would be much better than lunch. Just running buddies—just comfortable with each other. "Maybe we could run together."

Those pale eyebrows of hers drew to a straight line. "Oh, I don't know...."

"I could use the workout." He put on what he hoped was an engaging smile.

She continued to hesitate. "The testing room is full of exercise equipment. You could hop on a treadmill or stair stepper."

"I'd rather be outside. You could show me a good route."

She bit her lip, then shrugged. "Okay."

Her pace was faster than he expected. Lucky for him, he'd kept up his mileage, even during all the hassles of his move to California. The wide, linked roads of the many industrial parks made flat running paths. Flat paths made for casual, get-acquainted exchanges.

A warm breeze hit his face, carrying the smell of asphalt and ocean. He breathed in with deep satisfaction. "This is why I came to California." Detroit had held the spoiled smell of a failed marriage.

Flap, slap, flap. Her feet moved against the pavement. Her mouth didn't move at all.

He tried again. "The smell of the ocean. Good weather." Another pause that she didn't fill. "What about you? Do you like California?"

At that moment of required response, a group of four, running in the opposite direction, loomed in front of them. Cheerful hellos, shoulder shifting and the group passed.

So did another opportunity to get Carly talking.

"Sea and sun brought me here," Mack tried again, then grimaced. Even for a new transplant, discussing Southern California weather was becoming stale. "Yeah, and a couple of offers I couldn't refuse. Cycle Software was one, of course. And then my father decided to become part of my household. He retired from a vet practice last year and gave in to the lure of milder winters."

Had he put her to sleep? But no, beside him her ponytail bobbed with her acknowledging nod, and her feet were still moving.

He breathed in deeply and caught a bit of her delicate perfume in his lungs. His gaze drifted to admire the smooth tautness of her muscled legs.

She glanced his way, and he quickly redirected his stare. A second passed and then he turned his gaze to her face. Their eyes met briefly—involuntary messages flying both ways—then hers cut away from him to study the blacktop ten feet ahead. *Too late.* That something, the *tenseness,* between them was back.

Hell. His imitation of the weather channel anchorman wasn't working. Details of his decision to come to California? Duds, too. Nothing was dissipating the inappropriate, yet obviously unignorable, chemistry between them.

Bringing it into the open might help. He took a breath. "Maybe we should talk about this."

It was as if she was a fire he'd jabbed to life with a poker. An animated—and absolutely fake—smile plastered over her face. "California. I like it. Always liked California," she said quickly. "I'm from Indiana. My mother's still there, in the small town where I grew up. In the house where I grew up. Went to college at Cal Poly. I have an aunt on this coast. For some reason got it in my mind to see her. And the ocean. And palm trees. Without the palm tree thing, maybe I'd have headed for the East Coast. But those palm trees. Of course, I could have gone to Florida. My grandparents live in Florida. But at eighteen—"

"Hey, Carly!" A hail came from across the street. A woman, running in the opposite direction, yelled out to Carly about a 10K race the following weekend.

Carly turned and ran backward several paces, to discuss the possibilities of participating and to shout encouragement to the other woman.

Mack used the moments to process the everything and nothing that had just poured out of Carly. By the time she turned back, her face flushed and her smile a more natural one, he'd only reached the part about where she went to college.

He tried restarting the discussion his way. "What I meant we should talk about is—"

This time, she didn't even take a breath before interrupting. "I lived in the dorms the first two years. I met three other girls and in my junior year we…"

Mack tuned out this next round of Carly trivia. Tendrils of hair had escaped her ponytail, and he watched them bounce against the pale, fine skin of her nape. It wasn't that he wasn't interested in her life. He was too interested. He was too fascinated by the amazing, gossamer texture of her hair. Of the freckle on the rim of one ear. Of how—and why—she was so determined to avoid talking about the attraction between them.

She'd finished recounting her college studies and was on to the résumé-level details of her senior internship. At the cul-de-sac drive of an immense industrial park, she interrupted herself to remark, "Halfway point," as they made the circle and headed back in the direction they'd come.

Finally, after detailing how she'd found the job at Cycle Software, her conversation drifted off. Maybe she figured he knew the rest from her personnel file. Maybe she'd talked herself into feeling safe.

He took her long-winded hint and didn't try bringing up the subject again. He was feeling safer, too. Unintended—no, make that *untended*—attractions easily died off. Already there was less between them. And if he was eyeing her legs again, he thought, it was purely on a clinical basis. They'd traveled at a brisk pace for probably two and a half miles and she appeared almost as fresh as when they started.

"Is that what you do on the weekends?" he asked, remembering her conversation with the other woman earlier. "Run 10K races?" Innocuous, neutral conversation.

"Sometimes. I used to…know a little girl. I volunteered a lot with her Brownie troop." A bead of sweat, like a tear, rolled from the hair at her temple down her cheek. She lifted her arm to rub her face against the short sleeve of her shirt. "But I'm not doing that anymore."

As if still afraid of what might be said in the brief silence that followed, she spoke quickly again. "What about you? How do you spend your free time?"

"Free time?" He raised his eyebrows and grinned. "You've been to my house. Do you expect I have free *time?* Nanoseconds, maybe. That's when I practice my French braiding or try to jam Barbie into a party dress."

She laughed and he barely noticed the small, small dimple in her left cheek. She'd been right after all. They didn't need to acknowledge the attraction. Already he could tell she felt more comfortable with him, more familiar.

So he didn't need to confront her. To state the obvious. To make clear that she needn't worry because there was no room in his life for a female other than Kimmy. To explain how cynical he'd become about relationships between men and women.

Every day of his life he was a father, a son, a businessman, a homeowner, a pet owner. He didn't want the additional burden of this damn attraction, let alone a relationship.

It seemed now it wouldn't be an issue. A spurt of relief lightened his feet. "Race you to the corner," he challenged, grinning at her.

She took off first, without even answering. He gave chase, trailing behind her valentine red shorts and flag of curly hair.

He let her win, he felt that relieved.

At the corner, they bent, palms on their knees, breathing deeply. The back of her T-shirt clung damply to her fragile shoulder blades. A car breezed by, a white, only-in-California convertible, playing a song he hadn't heard in eighteen years.

And just like that he was fourteen again. At the city park a block and half from his boyhood home. That same song playing, about a beach baby, and he was holding the hand of his very first girlfriend.

The moment was crystal clear in his mind. The scent of the girl's herbal shampoo, the warmth of the sun on his face, the wetness between their pressed-together palms, the absolute conviction he'd had that he would live forever, that love would last forever, that people would make promises like marriage vows and parent-hood and never break them.

Carly looked up. That fake smile was gone. Her ear-lier nervousness left behind. She was just a woman, comfortable in her own skin, comfortable in his pres-ence.

Just what he'd aimed for, right?

Right.

He straightened, shifting his shoulders and shuffling his feet.

Her gaze narrowed. "You feel okay? Something the matter?"

Could he tell the truth? That he was suddenly itchy? Edgy?

"You look like you've seen a ghost," she said, her dimple winking.

"Ah. More like I heard one. That song." He gestured vaguely toward the car in the distance. "Takes me back."

Her pale eyebrows rose.

He couldn't answer the unspoken question. He couldn't think, not when he was noticing the light brightening her gray-green eyes like sunshine warming a still pool. Not when he was watching her uneven breaths raising the—don't even think the word—*woman parts* beneath her shirt.

They'd be dusted with freckles, too—wouldn't they? *God.*

"You're sure you're okay?"

"Fine," he answered instead of confessing to her that the attraction was back, bubbling like a vengeance in his blood.

Something else was back, too, something deeper, something that had been gone longer, that was reminiscent of sunshine and sweaty palms and an adolescent belief in the staying power of love.

Yeah. He was itchy. Edgy. Uncomfortable. All the things he'd hoped to ease in her.

"He's a bit older than you, dear, did I mention that?" Carly's mother's voice sounded girlish and excited. "Early forties. Maybe mid-forties."

"Uh-hmm." In pajamas and under the covers of her bed, Carly pinned the phone tighter between her ear and shoulder and dipped the brush back into the fingernail polish.

"But so handsome. I found out why he's just now getting his first church."

Carly held her breath as she painted the pinky nail of her right hand.

"Well?" Carly's mother prompted. "Don't you want to know?"

Whew. Only one minor overswipe. "Sure, Mom."

There was a dramatic pause. "He was in the *marines.*" She said the word reverently.

When Carly didn't immediately respond, she heard her mother's minihuff. "Don't you have anything to say?" she asked.

Carly laughed. "Mom, it's *you* that has the thing for men in uniform. How many times have you seen *An Officer and a Gentleman?* How about *Top Gun?*"

Her mother sighed. At forty-six, widow Laurie Carrothers appreciated a handsome man. "Don't forget *A Few Good Men.* Jack Nicholson looked wonderful in that."

"What did I tell you?" Carly laughed again.

"Well, how come you're not as enthusiastic as you were over the weekend? Pastor Hawkins is perfect for you."

"Mom, you know I'm not *really* counting on marrying him, right?"

Her mother's voice was stubborn. "I know it's time

you settled down, and you'll settle better back here in Spenser.''

''I hope you're right.''

''Of course I'm right. You go to the Heartland for matters of the heart.'' Carly imagined her mother's satisfied nod. ''Now tell me about this temporary boss of yours.''

Temporary. ''I went running with him yesterday. Nice guy. Good runner.''

As if that was all she'd noticed. But she clamped down on her wayward thoughts. The run *had* been pleasant. At first she'd worried he wanted to discuss that silly, *mild* awareness she had of him—how embarrassing!—but the conversation remained innocuous. She could feel relieved. Safe even.

Most likely her attraction to him was one-sided. Ignorable.

Her mother started talking again, but a call-waiting click signaled another caller for Carly. She quickly wrapped up the conversation with her mother—they'd chatted more than enough—and pressed the button to take the call.

It was Mack.

Carly hastily checked the time, after 10 p.m., and wondered what couldn't wait until morning.

''Kimmy accidentally played 'Fifty-Two Pickup' with the pages of the user's manual for the treadmill. I wanted to get through it tonight but I'm lost.''

Carly frowned. ''You can't put the pages back in order?''

''It's a *draft*. Documentation told me this copy didn't

have page numbers, but Big Bad Boss said 'no problem.'"

Now that she felt safe with him, she couldn't prevent her grin. "What did Big Bad Dad say to Kimmy?"

There was a long silence. "Okay. So you found me out. Kimmy isn't responsible at all. I knocked it off the counter chasing Corndog around the kitchen."

She *tsked*, laughed at her mental image of him running after the dog again, then finished painting the nails of her right hand as she talked him through reorganizing the document.

After a few minutes, he groaned.

"What now? You didn't drop it again, did you?"

"I just caught sight of the time. I didn't realize I called so late."

"That's okay, I was already on the phone," she said.

A brief silence. "I hope I didn't interrupt... anything."

"Nope, just my mother," she said cheerfully. "She's a night owl so you spared me, actually."

"What kind of bird are you?"

Carly jumped. Warm intimacy had entered his voice.

Ignoring the hubba-hubba reaction of her pulse, she cleared her throat. "The kind that needs her sleep before work tomorrow."

"Right." His voice matched her briskness. "So what's it going to cost me to keep my little fib about Kimmy quiet, Ms. Carrothers?"

Match his humor, she commanded herself. "Just your promise to stop blaming everything on the women in your life." She made a grand gesture, nearly knocking over the bottle of fingernail polish. "Yikes!"

"Everything okay?"

"Just a whoops. Almost spilled—" she squinted at the small printing on the bottle "—'Passion' all over the bedsheets."

A silence. "Bedsheets?" he asked, his voice deeper. "Passion?"

With just those words, the call changed. Business and humor fled, leaving only something else behind.

She laughed nervously. "That sounded weird, huh?"

Another small pause. "Weird wasn't my first thought."

I'm weak, Carly accused herself. *Only marshmallow strong.*

Because she liked the huskiness of his voice. It had been so long since she'd held the phone to her ear and heard a man's warmth and sexiness directed toward her. But the sexiness and the weakness were dangerous.

With effort, she straightened her spine against the pillows. "I—"

"I wanted to talk about this before," he interrupted. "This...what happens between us."

Clutching the bottle of polish, Carly fell back into the pillows. Oh, boy. "I don't think that's such a good idea."

His voice notched deeper. "You know what I'm talking about?"

Of course she knew.

What made men incapable of taking a hint? They didn't get it, whether it regarded what you truly wanted for your birthday or that you didn't want to acknowledge an attraction because it would make it that much harder to resist.

"It's fingernail polish, a color called 'Passion.' I nearly dumped it on my comforter," she said, trying to redirect him one more time.

He acted as if he didn't hear her. "At first, ignoring it seemed the best idea. But on the other hand, we *could* do something about it. Nothing serious, though. Just…play."

Play. The word was like hot sidewalk to her nerve endings. They hopped and danced. She swallowed. "Play?"

"I'm willing."

"Willing?" Her voice came out a high-pitched squeak. The idea of playing with the dark, hard-muscled Mack was electrifying. Squeak-ifying.

"As long as I'm sure nobody would be hurt. We could agree it's just for laughs," he said.

Tension ran like a slow finger down her back. He wasn't just talking about the awareness between them. Now he wanted to do something about it.

He was talking about a flirtation. Maybe something more. But she had only a few more weeks in California, and in the end, someone would be hurt.

There were pets and grandfathers and small girls to consider. Who would end up in the most pain? The answer was easy and came straight out of her past.

She would.

Carly sighed. No sense asking for trouble. Play? Nuh-uh. "I think I'll just skip my turn," she said. "It'll be safer that way."

I'll be safer that way.

3

— ▸ ◂ —

Determined to come up with a plan to deal with his latest problem with Carly, Mack took Corndog on his morning walk. The Lab pulled at the leash, and Mack reflexively tugged the puppy back to his side with a stern, "Heel." One driveway ahead, a rubber banded newspaper splatted against the cement. The *thwak* and the rumble of the paper carrier's van echoed inside his aching and plan-empty skull.

Coffee. Somebody in the blue house on the corner was brewing it, and he had to restrain himself from barging into their kitchen and demanding a cup.

He should have gone to bed earlier.

As in before he phoned Carly.

While the call had taken place around ten, he'd lain awake thinking about it for another few hours.

"Stupid." Corndog looked up at him expectantly, and Mack gave the dog a reluctant smile. "Not you, pup. Me."

Some stupid combination of long hours, his for-once-quiet household, talk of passion and sheets had brought about a phone flirtation. Mild. Just a toe in the water, but stupid all the same.

Hadn't he told himself during their run—hell, for the

past three years—that he didn't need another woman in his life? Kimmy, with her lace and bows, hairdos and dolls, was enough female for him. For God's sake, he'd had to bring in his father to handle the overload.

He turned the last of his block's corners, and his arm strained as Corndog smelled the metaphoric barn door. In the kitchen, the puppy scrabbled over the hardwood floor toward Cookies and Milk, Mack's father's furry companions. The older dogs patiently sat through Corndog's snuffling of their noses and necks. Corndog always gave them the once-over after his walk, as if they had been out in the world instead of him.

"Daddy!" With a squeal, Mack's own nose-and-neck snuffler jumped into his arms.

Growling like a grizzly, he gave her a big "bear" squeeze and carried her toward the countertop and the coffeemaker. To Kimmy's endless chatter—"A big spider in my dream, Daddy. Purple and yellow and wearing a *george*-ous sunhat"—he began making breakfast.

Well, Cheerios and toaster waffles. Mack looked over at his daughter, who was momentarily silenced by a large cereal spoon. He had only seconds to think before she started talking again. Closing his eyes, he gulped from his mug of coffee. *What to do about Carly?*

Too late. Cereal bite half chewed, Kimmy started on a description of something she'd seen "the other to-day"—yesterday—at preschool. Somebody had a *george*-ous backpack. Minnie dancing with Tigger. Purely feminine speculation entered her eyes as she batted too-adorable lashes his way.

"You have your own nice backpack," he said quickly. Before she could exert more of her wiles on him, the sound of Sinatra filled the house. "My Way." Cookies and Milk hauled themselves to their feet and Corndog did the psychodog dash around the kitchen table.

Mack's dad, Ray, entered the kitchen. Grits the cat trailed behind him.

Mack eyed the cat suspiciously. The President was still unaccounted for.

"Morning, Dad."

"Son." Ray made the rounds, kissing Kimmy on her head, ruffling the fur of Cookies and Milk, even managing a swipe at the endlessly dashing Corndog before he headed to the pantry and served each dog their morning meal.

Grits looked on the gobbling canines with disdain then elegantly nibbled a bite of his own breakfast. His tail swished as if clearing the air of a noxious odor.

Kimmy started hinting about the backpack and batting her eyelashes again. And though his daughter looked nothing like the gossamer blond, angel-kissed Carly, his thoughts returned to his assistant. What was he going to say to her this morning?

Sinatra crooned, the dogs scampered about with after-breakfast enthusiasm, Grits acted as if they were best friends and began to tarantella with his ankles. Kimmy chattered. Chattered. Chattered.

Mack squeezed shut his eyes, trying to think. He held the coffee mug beneath his nose for inspiration.

Nothing.

Nothing?

Nothing. He needn't say anything. She'd made it clear she wasn't interested. He'd make it clear he wasn't devastated. That he wasn't affected at all.

How simple.

Grits yowled at him. Mack looked down. The cat blinked one eye, then the other.

That reminded him of The President. They'd thought finding the snake would be simple, too.

Carly looked back at her apartment before shutting and locking the door. Even without a single box packed, the place seemed empty. Maybe it was because of her avowed intention to leave.

Liar. The apartment had seemed devoid of life since Laurel stopped coming there. The little girl had always left something of herself at Carly's—a library book, a sweatshirt. Carly had never returned the item until the next visit, instead smiling whenever she caught sight of a *Bobbsey Twins* paperback or "Kirby School Cougars" on a blue pullover.

As she did at least once each day, Carly paused and whispered a little prayer for Laurel. She wanted the girl to be safe, happy, loved. And with the remarriage of her mother and father, Carly felt sure she was.

With Laurel checked off Carly's mental list, she could worry about Mack.

A spurt of anger quickened her pace to her car. Darn him. If he hadn't gone all husky and playful the night before, she might have her reaction to him under control.

Extinguished.

But no, that teasing conversation had ignited a flash

fire of renewed response. If he gave her another one of those dangerous grins today, it would serve him right if she melted all over his shoes.

Which she wouldn't, of course.

He'd offered. She'd rebuffed. They needn't refer to the conversation again.

She only had to make it through that first glance without doing something embarrassing, like blushing or blurting out she'd changed her mind.

Okay, maybe she had to make it through more than a glance. The first ten minutes.

Oh, darn, get serious. The whole day had potential for embarrassment. But if they could just make it through eight to five, as professionals, as friendly but distant co-workers, then all the other days would be easy.

Piece of cake.

Simple.

Through the open door of his office, Mack could hear the lead team members of the new treadmill project cajoling Carly.

"Come on," said Gary, the frizzy-headed programmer with the athlete's build. "You know I'd do it, but my knees are shot."

Bruce, pale and slight, chimed in. "Yeah, come on. I'd do it, but unfortunately I picked today to have quadruple-caffeine cola and chocolate cupcakes for breakfast."

Carly wasn't buying any. "Bruce, that's your morning menu *every* day."

Mack could hear the practiced remorse in the other

man's voice. "Exactly why we need you on the machine, Carly. Don'tcha want to see what we made it do?"

"Can't you wait until this afternoon?"

Cycle employed a couple of college kids in the afternoons to test the software. Under the programmers' direction they'd use the treadmill, rowing machine, stair stepper or bicycle.

"Please, Carly." Gary tried again.

"Oh, all right," she said. But she didn't sound that put out. Mack wondered if she was glad for an excuse to avoid him a while longer.

That morning he'd caught a glimpse of the ruffling hem of her skirt as she'd ducked into her office when he'd walked down the hall. She'd been engrossed in a phone call when he'd glanced in.

Later he thought he saw her heading to the water cooler, but when she spied him filling his glass, she'd spun in the opposite direction.

Thinking it best to postpone their meeting himself, he'd left her alone.

But now the treadmill programmers had coaxed her into the testing room. There were bound to be several other people around while she tested the program. Perfect timing.

He'd go in and watch what they were doing. As head of Cycle Software, he needed briefing on the latest developments. And he'd prove to Carly there was nothing to feel awkward about.

He gave them about twenty minutes prep time, then slipped in the testing room and took a seat at the back, behind a couple of exercise bicycles.

Nobody noticed him. Gary and Bruce flanked the test treadmill, while Carly, dressed in sky blue shorts and tank top, stood on the unmoving tread. A couple of other programmers and the office manager, Lisa, also hovered about.

In front of the treadmill was a three-by-four-foot movie-type surround screen, the basis of Cycle's newest treadmill software product. A small projector was hidden in the treadmill's frame. At the user's direction, it would project a moving image on the vertical screen.

During testing, wires ran from the treadmill frame's face to a PC tower on a nearby desk. Bruce trotted over to the tower and thumbed through a stack of CDs on the desktop. "Big Sur? Autumn in Vermont? Or our personal favorite, Deserted Mexican Beach?"

"Surprise me," Carly said.

Bruce and Gary exchanged amused glances. "Oh, we will."

"I'll tell The Dominatrix you're here," Bruce said, fiddling with the keyboard as Carly conversed quietly with Lisa.

The new treadmill product was based on Cycle's supremely popular "Virtual Trainer" software. When a password was keyed in on the treadmill's face, the chip inside the treadmill—known affectionately around Cycle as "The Dominatrix" for her sexy voice and sadomasochistic tendencies—would know the user and the user's exercise patterns and goals. She then would direct the user's workout, controlling the intensity, speed and length.

The Dominatrix worked similarly for a rowing machine, stair stepper, exercise bicycle and treadmill. But

Cycle was about to add a new feature for that last piece of equipment.

"All set," Bruce called out.

The tread started moving. A sultry voice emanated from the speaker on the treadmill. "Hi, Carly. Welcome to your fantasy workout."

Carly, walking to keep up with the treadmill, grimaced. "'Fantasy workout'? Gimme a break, guys."

Gary waved away the concern. "We can change what she says. Just watch." He pointed toward the screen.

An image appeared. Even though he knew what was supposed to happen, Mack's breath caught as an endless beach was projected on the screen. Waves rushed toward the sand. Birds flew overhead. And he could hear them. The *shush* of the water. The screech of the gulls. It should be even better for Carly, with the screen tilted for her line of sight and the sounds reaching her ears first.

The image moved at the same pace as the tread, making her feel like she was running on that endless, private Mexican beach. Palms swayed to the left. A sandpiper ran across the sand. The only thing missing was the smell of ocean and a real breeze.

But this should be enough to entice the most bored of exercise enthusiasts.

Carly was jogging at an easy pace, gaze glued to the screen. Her taut legs moved smoothly, almost mesmerizing Mack with their rhythm.

Another sandpiper raced by. Carly looked away from the moving image, a grin digging that incredible dimple in her left cheek. "This is great, guys!" She high-fived Gary.

With Carly relaxed and happy, Mack thought it the perfect time to inject his professional presence.

Show her that last night meant nothing.

He rose from his place and strode toward the group around the treadmill. "I like it," he said. "Good job, everybody."

Several sets of startled eyes swung his way.

Carly missed a step and bobbled. His hand shot out to steady her.

Carly felt Mack's hand close over her upper arm like a sizzling lick of lightning. She stumbled again, and his other hand touched her waist.

Lightning? It felt more like thunder, Carly thought, with her heart pounding *boom boom boom* in her chest.

It's the first time he's touched me.

"I'm okay now," she managed to force out, and his hands fell away. Desperate to make sure no one else had noticed her embarrassing response—just what she'd hoped to avoid today—she looked around the small circle of co-workers, her legs regaining the slow pace.

Though everybody else appeared normal, Bruce's and Gary's faces looked really weird. Had they noticed her reaction to Mack? Maybe she should stop the test. After a shower and in her business clothes, she'd have a better chance of reacting professionally toward him.

She pasted on a cheerful smile. "All done, guys?"

Bruce's posture relaxed. "Yeah, yeah. Let's finish this up another time." He hurried toward the PC tower.

"No." Mack spoke firmly. "I want to see the whole run." He looked at Carly. "Unless you're too tired."

Two of his fingers touched the back of her hand, where it gripped the treadmill's handlebar. Heat rose up her neck. *Darn.* The man's touch was like a cattle prod. She swallowed. "I can go on." Wasn't that the professional response?

Over Mack's head, Carly caught sight of Gary's frantic hand signals. She grimaced. What was he trying to tell her? "Take the speed down, will you, Bruce?"

At Gary's eye roll, she hastily changed her mind. "I mean speed it up."

Gary rolled his eyes again. Staring at him, she shrugged a bit, to indicate her confusion. Then Mack touched her hand, distracting her, dizzying her again, and she tried to ignore the sensation as she answered his crisp questions about the experience of the "fantasy" run.

Another mile of beach passed. Enthusiasm in his voice, Mack pointed out two dolphins playing in the waves. He touched her arm again, and her stomach jumped and twirled in time with the leaping pair.

When she could breathe once more, she looked over at Bruce and Gary. Those funny expressions were etched deeper onto their faces, and she tried figuring out what they wanted her to do.

"Getting tired?" Mack asked.

From behind his back, Bruce and Gary nodded, their heads bobbing emphatically.

"Yes?" Carly replied, one eye on Bruce and Gary. The head bobbing recurred and their faces split in relieved smiles. Bruce made another move toward the PC.

"Wait." Mack pointed toward the screen.

Carly leaned forward. Something appeared in the distance on the beach. She squinted. A pair of runners?

She looked at Gary. "You guys didn't tell me about meeting other runners along the way."

Gary stared down at the floor as if he wished it would develop a man-sized hole. "Uh...it's just something we're playing around with."

"Yeah," Bruce added nervously. "We were thinking maybe famous sports figures could join the user on the run. You know, give a pep talk."

"Good idea. Let's discuss it with Marketing." Mack rubbed his jaw, his gaze still on the screen. "So who's that?"

The running pair were still at squint distance.

The Dominatrix's silky voice spoke over the crashing waves. "Carly, didn't I promise you a fantasy? It lies just ahead."

The Dominatrix's words, something about the nearing couple, and Bruce and Gary's notorious penchant for practical jokes suddenly synthesized in Carly's mind.

She didn't want to see what lay ahead. Nuh-uh. No way.

Mack drew closer to her as he tried to get the same view of the screen as she. His breath washed across the skin of her arm, prickling it.

"I need to stop, Bruce," Carly said abruptly. The couple was coming nearer and nearer. She recognized herself, in the red shorts and T-shirt she'd run in the other day. And Mack, too, of course, looking strong and delicious.

"You guys filmed us." Mack's brow furrowed. "But how'd you get us on the beach?"

Gary shrugged uneasily. "A little bit of this, a little bit of that. I have a buddy who does computer animation for the movies."

"I want to get off now, Bruce." Mack might think all the prankster programmers had up their sleeves was a little run on the beach, but Carly knew them better. *Computer animation, fantasy.* Those words echoed in her skull.

"I want to see this." With that, Mack hopped on the treadmill.

Oh, shoot. Behind her, his chest facing her back, he kept pace with her. The tread moved just as smoothly with his extra weight as they drew inexorably closer to their own image.

"Strange, huh?" Mack spoke in her ear. "Us approaching…us."

The flesh behind Carly's ear goose bumped. Even stranger is the word *us.* But determined to hold on to every ounce of professionalism, she stayed silent and straightened her spine to avoid any touch of the man behind her.

And just then, their nearing images halted.

Oh, no.

Gary must've gotten a lot of help from his computer animation buddy. Because, when the real Carly and Mack were about thirty feet away, the computerized Carly and Mack turned to each other…wrapped their arms around each other à la *Gone with the Wind*…

Kissed.

* * *

Mack pulled a pen from the purple-glazed pencil cup Kimmy had made for him and tried tuning out the vigorous thumps, clumps and *ping-ping-ping* generated by the construction crew.

Following a quiet morning, the workers had arrived after lunch and spent the entire afternoon working directly above the Cycle Software offices.

Wonk-whack.

Directly above his office.

He checked his watch. Nearly 6:00 p.m., and the crew showed no sign of letting up. Maybe, like him, for all their bluster they hadn't made much progress this afternoon.

Yeah, he'd been blustering since the, uh, on-screen kiss. Bruce and Gary, obviously worried, had made abject apologies to both him and Carly. Once Mack laughed, so had everyone else. Hell, he could take a joke with the best of them.

But he hadn't done more than five minutes in a row of productive work since this morning. As of fifteen minutes before, everyone else at Cycle had left, even Bruce and Gary, who usually worked odd hours. Mack thought he could finally strike back at the piles warring on his desk.

And quit thinking about Carly.

Her cheeks flushed, that incredibly surprising dimple, the sensation of her skin beneath his hand.

He hadn't been able to stop himself from touching her again. And then again.

Jabbing his pen back in the blob, he rested his head

against the chair. What had Carly thought about that kiss?

Probably nothing, he told himself ruthlessly. She'd chuckled along with him and shaken a finger at Bruce and Gary with a promise to get back at them. Then she'd gone to shower in the women's rest room and ended up back in her skirt and blouse, working all afternoon in her office as if her lips had never touched his.

Which they never had, of course.

A *whack-thonk* sounded right above his head, quickly overlaid by a *tap-tap-tap*. Mack sighed, wishing the noise away.

Tap-tap-tap.

"Mack?" Carly's voice.

Opening his eyes, he realized she'd been knocking on his door. He straightened in the chair. "Come in, I thought everyone was gone."

She walked hesitantly into the room, carrying her purse, obviously on her way out.

"And I thought your knocking," he continued, jabbing his thumb in the direction of the roof, "was just another hello from the guys upstairs."

She half smiled and came a few more steps forward.

That's right, he told himself. Put her at ease. Nothing had changed since this morning's resolve. You're still unaffected, even by a kiss you *didn't* really experience.

"What can I do for you?" he asked.

She opened her mouth just as a *clank* rattled the walls. Shaking his head, Mack put up a hand, then quickly moved from his chair and grabbed his briefcase to stuff a few things inside. When the echoing noise diminished, he looked at Carly.

"I'm going home," he said over the continued bumps and bangs. "Can I walk you out?"

In the parking lot, one exit was blocked by a massive crane in the process of lifting a steel beam into place. Men in hard hats swarmed all over the building, shouting instructions to one another. But at Carly's car, away from the noise, at least they could hear each other speak.

Mack leaned against the driver's door. "This is better."

Carly's hand fluffed nervously through her hair. Not in the usual tight twist, the curls fell softly toward her shoulders. "I wanted to talk to you about Bruce and Gary." She touched her hair again. "I hope you know they didn't mean any harm."

Remembering the odd feeling of watching himself kiss her sent flashes of heat from his brain southward. "No big deal."

She grimaced. "You see, we do that kind of stuff to each other all the time. Pranks."

He grimaced back. "Do I look like somebody who can't take a joke? Nobody's in any trouble."

Her shoulders finally relaxed. "I told them…"

His eyes narrowed. "You told them?"

She shrugged. "Bruce and Gary thought you looked a little…" She shrugged again. "I told them you didn't look mad to me."

Right. I wasn't mad. I was unaffected. Unbothered. "No big deal," he said again.

She shrugged another time. "Well, good."

"Good."

Okay, so it was bad! Okay, so it pissed him off that they'd animated a damn kiss that he'd never experienced. And it was even more frustrating that she was standing there, and another one of those damn curls of hers was tickling the corner of her mouth, just like he wanted to.

To control the mental outburst, Mack inhaled a deep breath. He should move. He was blocking the door to her car, and she was probably wondering when he was going to get out of her way.

Except that she wasn't looking at the door at all. Or really, even, at him. She was looking at his mouth.

Her tongue came out and licked her bottom lip. And on that lip, at the edge of the center, fat, kissable part, rested a gold freckle. He thought of Tinkerbell and pixie dust and then Kimmy, but not one of the thoughts distracted him from what he wanted.

He wanted that kiss.

The one on the beach. Now that he'd seen it, surely it was owed to him. Belonged to him.

He didn't take his gaze off her mouth. "Carly?" The word came out hoarse.

"Um?" He had no idea where she was looking, but she sounded as distracted as he.

Maybe he should explain how he felt about the kiss. Explain how he understood that she'd expressed her disinterest last night, but now there was that kiss between them that really was his to take.

He shifted his gaze from her mouth to her eyes, hoping to gauge the reception of such an admittedly illogical explanation.

Her eyes were still on *his* mouth.

Suddenly something clicked into place. Like a latch catching on a fine, thin cable that linked him to her.

"Do I have to explain this?" he asked.

"Explain what?" She lifted her gaze to his.

And then that cable between them pulled taut, humming like a guitar string, reverberating with each of their breaths.

"About the kiss," he said quickly, because time was running out. "That I'm going to kiss you."

Her eyelashes fluttered down against her pixie-dusted cheeks and her face tilted toward his. "No," she said.

Sounds receded. He drew toward her mouth, anticipation tightening that linking cable one more notch.

His fingers shook as they closed on her shoulders, and the feel of her beneath his hands made him hard.

His mouth brushed hers. In the distance, men's voices, shouting. Like a whole locker room full of guys cheering him on.

He went for more this time. His lips, hard against hers.

Softness. Sweet breath. Heat tightening his groin.

She kissed back.

And then the earth moved....

Literally moved.

4

A steel girder had crashed through the roof of the building housing Cycle Software, destroying most of the third floor.

The next morning, as Carly stepped out of the shower, she relived her shock and the expression of stunned surprise on Mack's face. After drying off, Carly inspected herself in the full-length mirror. She looked tired. The construction accident had kept them on-site until well past dark, and then she'd come home to make a long round of phone calls.

With a sigh, she scoured her closet for possibilities. "Boring black or banal beige?" she asked her reflection, holding two business suits against her body. Her reflected image didn't bother answering, obviously aware there was no established etiquette for the situation.

Because not only was she going to work today with the man who'd kissed her last night—don't think about the kiss, don't think about the kiss—but she was going to be working with him *alone,* in his home.

After an exchanged what-the-heck-do-we-do-now look, she and Mack had used the cell phone in his car to contact John. In that competent CEO way of his,

John had taken the news with aplomb. He didn't want to seek new office space until his return from Europe, so after appointing one administrative team, he'd left it to that aforesaid team to break the rest of the staff into small product groups that could work from their homes.

She stared into her reflected face, absently noting her hair frothing more wildly than usual. *Not* a bad hair day, too. Sigh.

The beige had to go. She dropped the dress and jacket combo and considered the severe lines of the black. Damn her conscience. Damn her loyalty. Without those two bedrocks she wouldn't be diving into the pool of Working With the Kissable Boss.

Don't think about the kiss, don't think about the kiss.

Think instead about the ear-splitting crash the steel beam had made last night. How lucky she and Mack were to be out of the building. How incredibly lucky that no one else was hurt.

And how all that incredible luck only extended so far.

Everybody—reached last night by phone—was oh so flexible about working from home. Thought the product groups a sound idea. Lisa, the office manager, promised to locate and provide equipment and software files from the off-site backup vault. Leaving the administrative team to put out fires, smooth waters and prepare for an important trip at the end the month.

And here's where that luck ran out—that administrative team was none other than the new president, Mack, and his just-kissed assistant, Carly.

You were not supposed to think about the kiss!

Yet even under its influence, her conscience and her loyalty to John and Cycle Software had not allowed her to walk away from the company when facing this new crisis. Oh, no, instead she had nodded and agreed and planned and agreed, all that agreeing taking her to this morning and this moment of boring black or banal beige to make the statement for her that *I'm here for working and not for kissing.*

Groan. The kiss again.

Not thinking about it was like being on a diet and trying to forget the box of extra-fudgy brownie mix in the cupboard. Just an egg, some oil and water, and whammo! brownies would arrive, hot and steamy and tasting so-o-o-o good, like that kiss—

Don't—

Oh, for gosh sake, go ahead and think about the kiss!

Carly smoothed panty hose up her thighs and allowed herself to remember his hard mouth, the little scratch his five-o'clock beard made against her chin, the heat on her cheeks as her senses exploded with the knowledge that this was *some kind of kiss.*

Okay. Fine. It was some kind of kiss. But acknowledging the fact didn't change that he was the wrong kind of man, that she was leaving in less than four weeks, and that in twenty minutes she should be facing him and getting down to work. Oh, no, it just made everything worse.

She sighed and wriggled into the skirt of the businesslike black suit. Her only option was to keep the relationship professional from now on.

Yeah, she would merely ignore that metaphoric pan of brownies.

Steaming.

Luscious.

Don't think about the kiss.

Securely zipped and buttoned in her businesslike black, Carly approached Mack's door. She'd agreed to work from his home because her condo was one-door-away-from-the-bedroom tiny and would be too chaotic as she packed up for her move. Mack's front doorbell rang loudly. When he pulled it open, a delicious smell wafted through the doorway.

Carly's heart jerked. "What's that smell?" she demanded.

Mack's eyebrows raised. "And good morning to you, too." He nodded back inside. "My father's baking."

With palms suddenly damp, she tightened her grip on her briefcase and the large shopping bag she carried, then crossed over the threshold. "Just tell me it isn't brownies."

Mack shrugged. "Something with chocolate. Is that a problem?"

Carly mutely shook her head. Professional. He's the boss and nothing more.

"Let me show you the way to my office, then." He looked skeptically at her business black. "I, uh, have to tell you it's not exactly ready for a suit and stockings."

"No problem." Carly waved off the concern and tried *not* to note the way Mack looked in a pair of worn blue jeans and a T-shirt advertising Miles for the Heart

10K Race. She also tried to ignore everything she passed on the way to the office.

Safer to see Mack as a boss, not as a man who left his front window curtainless—just as she would, to get the most of the view of the front yard—not as a man who chose for his living room big heavy furniture with appealing and oversize down-filled cushions. Not as a man who arranged family portraits in the hall and then, just as seriously, hung an off-kilter picture frame, cut from a paper plate. The paper plate frame bore a photo of a mugging Mack and Kimmy and was embellished by what looked suspiciously like dried macaroni.

She didn't pay attention to any of that, instead following Mack into a large, white-painted room with a window looking out toward the backyard and pool. Dropping her briefcase and bag, she raised her eyebrows. "When you said it wasn't ready for a suit and stockings, you meant it, didn't you?"

Along one wall was a large desk holding a phone, a shoe box and a thick layer of dust. Cardboard boxes, piled waist high and shoulder level, effectively blocked access to it as well as access to any other square foot of the room except for a small, cleared space by the door.

Mack grinned. "That's why I suggested Dad do something in chocolate."

Carly bumped against one of the box towers, noting with dismay the swath of dust the move left behind on her skirt. She swatted at the mark. "I'm going to need a dust cloth way before the chocolate."

"Sorry. We just keep piling stuff in here and shutting the door." Mack nudged a stack of boxes with his foot. "I think most of these are empty."

"All the easier to move, then." Carly gingerly picked up one of the boxes, holding it away from her chest. "Where to, boss?" She sneezed so violently she dropped the box, leaving another dirt swipe against her skirt. She groaned.

Mack frowned. "We've got to get you out of those clothes."

Carly shot him a look, but guessed only *she* heard the sexy implication. *Down, girl.* She brushed vigorously at her skirt. "You have something in a size seven?"

But his eyes were looking at her legs, and his mouth wasn't moving at all. Carly quickly looked down, and realized that during her attempts to clean her skirt, she'd managed to catch the hem and pull the normally knee-length hemline to midthigh—make that *mid*, midthigh. To top it off, a run in her stocking trailed down toward her ankle.

She froze. How embarrassing—but it wasn't. How messy she must look—but she knew he didn't see it that way. For an instant, with her skirt up and that run accentuating the length of her leg, Carly had a sensation of wantonness—of decadence.

How Mack was seeing her.

Carly swatted down the skirt, her face burning. "Oh, terrific. Um—"

"I need to get you something else to wear," he said quietly.

Carly didn't bother joking about a particular size this time. The intense look on Mack's face, the heat of her own, told her that the business black wasn't going to work. Not now. Not when she'd overlaid the look with a cheesecake image—however unintentional.

Minutes later, in another "10K" T-shirt—size XL— and a pair of drawstring, cutoff sweatpants, Carly felt much safer. Okay, so it wasn't the professional look, but who could think of anything *but* work when wearing a guy's athletic gear? The stuff smelled like laundry detergent and Mack.

But she didn't notice that. Instead, in bare feet, she tackled the cardboard towers, taking two or three empty boxes at a time to the garage. Even the visit from Grits the cat that reminded her of the missing snake—yes, still MIA according to Mack—and her terror of mice that might have found a home in the boxes couldn't persuade her to wear her black midheel pumps with gray sweats. Even a small-town girl had to show a smidgeon of fashion sense.

There were no interruptions—Kimmy attended preschool until lunch and Ray James was gardening in the backyard with the dogs—so by midmorning, they'd cleared most of the empty boxes out of the office. The room's closet had been located, and Mack had stashed a filing cabinet and a few of the filled boxes there. By eleven, they could finally approach the desk.

The phone rang.

Carly looked at Mack, knowing that phone was a separate, business-only line. Should she answer it? He looked back. It rang again. They both reached for the receiver, and Carly knocked the shoe box off the desk onto the floor.

With a grimace at the strewn contents, Carly grabbed the phone while Mack bent down to the spilled box.

After assuring Lisa that she would pick up some files from her during the lunch hour and avoiding several leading, teasing questions about her other team member, Carly hung up the phone feeling pretty proud of herself.

All things considered, the morning had gone fairly well. Even sans her business black, she'd kept things professional. Kept Mack a boss-distance away.

She turned toward him. Her boss had refilled the upturned box and set it back on the desk corner, with the exception of a small, framed photo he held in his hands. Out of friendly, employee-type curiosity, Carly peeped around him to take a look at it, and found herself staring into the cool eyes and tight smile of Mack's bride.

That's what it was. A wedding photo. Mack was in it, too, and it was one of those clasped-hands-cut-the-cake poses. He wore a dark suit and looked younger, tanner, more relaxed. Okay, happy even.

She—thin and brown-eyed—wore what appeared to be a white linen suit. Nothing covered her dark hair that hung smooth and straight to her shoulders. The cake was streamlined and elegant, too. No fresh flowers and sugary rosettes like Carly would have chosen, just a cool band of icing topped with a simple ribbon of silver.

Mack's hand moved against the frame—caressingly?—and his voice sounded distant. "I never know quite what to do with these things."

Carly swallowed. How should an employee respond? Was any response required?

"Throw them out? Pack them away?" His thumb moved restlessly over the corner of the frame.

Carly swallowed again. "Maybe you should save them for Kimmy."

"Why?" He didn't look at her when he asked.

"Little girls want to know about stuff like that. They like to dream about weddings. You know. Big bouquets and men in tuxedos and dresses with yards and yards of tulle. Gossamer veils...." Carly stopped, suddenly, excruciatingly aware that it looked like Mack and his ex-wife's wedding had been none of those things.

His wry smile said he noticed that, too. "I thought I was lucky, you know."

She wanted to rub the frown line between his brows away. "How do you mean?"

"No attendants. Justice of the peace. My best suit. I think ten people came to our reception." He looked away. "Maybe nine."

"It sounds...quiet." She hurriedly added, "Nice."

That wry smile again. "I'd been in about seven weddings that summer. Attended twenty-seven it seemed like. All my friends were complaining about monkey suits and diamond selection and table-seating etiquette. And all I had to do was show up with my tie knotted correctly and a plain gold band in my pocket."

Carly thought this wasn't the kind of stuff she wanted a boss to be telling her. "I'm sure that was a relief."

"Yeah, that's what I felt at the time. I thought I'd found a woman in a million."

Carly was fairly certain that little skip she felt in her stomach wasn't a wince. She was also fairly certain that she shouldn't touch him, which her hands were just aching to do.

"She said she didn't want any fuss," Mack went on, "and I thought that was great. Just great."

"Great," Carly echoed faintly, for lack of something better.

Suddenly he looked at her. Dark eyes slamming into her with direct force. "But I should have known, huh? A woman who doesn't like fuss? Mix that up with two demanding careers, a child, a grandfather, and what do you get?"

Mack tossed the frame into the box with such force that the box slid across the dusty surface of the desk. "Disaster."

Carly fisted her hands to keep from touching the tense line of his shoulders. Heat crawled up her neck again, and her cheekbones burned. "I'm sorry."

He shot her an unreadable look, then transferred his gaze out the window. Sunlight warmed the grass out there, but Carly knew he didn't see it. Birds, doing late-spring chores, crossed each other in the sky, but Carly knew Mack was seeing some other, darker time.

She shivered. Because he wasn't a boss anymore. Or the guy who'd kissed her crazy the day before. He was a man with regrets and disappointments—that baggage stuff she professed to disdain but that touched her heart, anyway.

She, a no-fuss woman herself.

At noon, driving Kimmy home from preschool, Mack figured he owed Carly an apology. The poor woman comes over to work on Cycle business and instead finds herself as: one, a moving company; two, a human dust rag; and three, worst of all, recipient of his personal bitterness.

In the rearview mirror, he could see that Kimmy had fallen asleep in her car seat. Preschool wore her out—thank God—and her chimp-level energy would require a reenergizing nap for the next couple of hours.

He didn't know why he'd unloaded on Carly. She'd looked so cute and prim in her basic black on his doorstep. Then so appalled when she'd caught him staring at her legs. Neither should have unleashed his talk about Suzanne. With a finger he notched down the air-conditioning. Just thinking about his ex-wife turned him colder.

So why had he said anything to Carly about her? An unconscious mistake? A *subconscious* warning?

Was he trying to tell Carly he wasn't a trusting man?

And just why would he do that?

Because of the kiss, you fool.

Because the kiss had been so damn powerful that he'd wanted to simultaneously run away…and take her with him.

He clicked the air-conditioning knob up two notches. It was getting hot in the car. Just as hot as the damn office, where all he could think about was the delicate run in her stockings that had traveled down her thigh, about how his T-shirt kept sliding to one side of her shoulder to play peekaboo with a shell pink bra strap, about how delicious and mesmerizing he found the fragrance of Carly's perfume.

Groaning, he pulled in the driveway. He'd better apologize. Now. Right away. For the kiss, too.

Not that it was anything he felt sorry for—hell no—but maybe an apology would sap the strength from the memory of it. Remind him of what a bad idea it was to keep thinking about doing it again. His life didn't need the added burden of a woman.

With Kimmy in his arms, he quietly shut the front door behind him and mounted the stairs to lay her on her canopied bed. Through her window, he could see his father sleeping on a lounge chair in the shade of the backyard, the dogs sprawled on the grass nearby.

Privacy assured, he could tell Carly he was sorry for spilling his guts about his former marriage. For a kiss that shouldn't have happened...and wouldn't happen again.

Approaching the half-open office door, he saw her sitting at the desk, her back to him, both hands flipping through two separate computer printouts. For a moment he thought she was talking to herself. "A bit more than three weeks," she said. "Then I'll be back in Indiana."

Another voice, though, a huskier replica of Carly's, answered. "I'm preparing your room, sweetie. Everything just the same."

Mack frowned. Ah. The speakerphone.

"*Mom.* Please remember I'm a grown woman now. And I won't be living at home permanently."

"I know, I know, that's why I left you the urgent message to call me."

Mack figured he should tiptoe away. Head for the kitchen and make a ham sandwich and a glass of milk.

Carly's mother continued. "Your minister said last

night he really wants to settle down. I've been telling him all about you."

Carly's *minister?* Mack tried to move his feet. They didn't obey.

"Mom—"

"Now just wait. I told him how you're tired of Los Angeles. How you wanted to come back to your small-town roots. He thought it was very admirable." She giggled. "I even showed him your picture, and he was nice enough to say we looked just like sisters."

"Way to go, Mom. But really, I know we've said he'd be a perfect husband for me, but that's—"

Mack couldn't hear the rest because "perfect husband" kept echoing in his brain. What the hell?

"You just come back to Indiana, Carly, and leave the matchmaking to me. Reverend Hawkins will be yours by the end of the summer."

He must have made some startled sound because suddenly Carly whirled and caught his eye through the half-open door. Whirling back, she picked up the receiver and hurriedly finished her call. Instinctively Mack stepped forward as if he hadn't been standing there eavesdropping for several moments. *Perfect husband?* The reverend would be Carly's by the end of the summer?

As he came in, she turned to him and gestured toward the phone. "Just a silly call from my mother." Red flags of color painted her cheekbones.

He was seeing red. He didn't know what made him madder—that she was quitting on him not for another position but to move to Indiana or that motivating her move was some saintly husband.

That she'd apparently never met before.

Certainly hadn't kissed him.

He wasn't apologizing. Hell, no. Not for anything. Especially not for that kiss.

After the lunch break, Carly's stomach had sunk and stayed there. Mack was back in the office, bringing with him a new, unexplainable unease. They'd moved a small table in and set up the fax machine, copier and computer there.

He was working at the terminal while she made a round of phone calls to the product teams to check on their progress. She clacked the receiver in its cradle and spoke to his unyielding spine. "Gary and Bruce are fine, too."

He grunted in response.

If only he'd *look* at her. Maybe that would ease the tension in the room. "I'm afraid to say I think they've got the Playboy Channel on, though. Some pretty strange moans and groans in the background."

He shot her a look. "You're kidding."

Carly shrugged, trying a smile. "They claim that cable TV is their inspiration. Think of The Dominatrix."

Ooops. That was a mistake. Because he *really* looked at her now and in his eyes was the memory of their virtual run on the virtual beach and their virtual kiss...and their real kiss. Carly shivered.

"It's hot in here," she said lamely, and crossed the room to open the window. A warm breeze brushed by her, ruffling some papers on the desk and blowing them to the ground.

Carly bent to retrieve them—and so did Mack. They

met knee to knee on the floor, their hands splayed against the papers. Her pinky finger brushed him. She jerked it away, but he just stretched his hand to capture her smallest finger beneath his.

"Carly," he said, his voice husky, "I have a confession to make."

Oh, no. This wasn't easing the tension. It shimmered between them like heat off the hood of a car in the intense California sunshine.

"Daddy!" A squealing mix of brown hair and flying limbs leaped from the doorway onto Mack's back.

"Ooof." His air whooshed out, and under Kimmy's impetus his head came forward and bonked Carly's.

They both sat back, rubbing their foreheads. Kimmy, undaunted, slid off her father's back and plopped onto his lap. "Whatcha doin', Dad?"

He smiled ruefully down at his daughter. Carly's heart did a little jump turn that she put down as reaction to the head bump.

"Working, little bug. Say hello to Ms. Carrothers."

Kimmy barely spared her a glance. "Hi-hi." She pushed the hair off her father's forehead. "Gimme something to eat, Daddy." Her palms cupped his cheeks and pushed.

Mack made an incredible-looking fish. But Carly paid little attention, instead gathering up the papers and sitting down at the desk.

"I hear Granddad in the kitchen, bug. He'll get you a snack. Ms. Carrothers and I are talk—working."

Kimmy skipped away, seemingly mollified. Mack looked back at Carly. "About that confession..."

Make that temporarily mollified. In an instant

Kimmy was back again, a plate of cookies in her hand and trailed by three dogs.

Carly didn't have time to decide if she welcomed the interruption or not. The big yellow Lab, Corndog, suddenly noticed that a stranger was in the house. Three feet from her he stilled, his lolling tongue in midswipe of Mack's hand.

Wary of strange dogs, Carly stilled, too.

Unnecessarily. Because with a joyous wriggle, Corndog bounded to her and started washing her hands, arms and chin with an ecstatic tongue. Even after Mack hauled him off, he came right back to her, flopping down on her bare feet and staring up at her with a "come hither and pet me" yearning in his eyes.

More sedately, the two older dogs approached, and she patted them, too.

All the while Kimmy chattered. About the snack at preschool. The book at circle time. How many twirls she'd accomplished on the tire swing.

Humming Sinatra's "Chicago," Ray James ambled into the room with a tray holding glasses of milk.

A few minutes later, with the delicious taste of chocolate cookies on her tongue, her ears filled with little-girl talk, her bare feet warmed by the yellow fur of Corndog, Carly met Mack's gaze.

That shimmering heat returned, and she gripped tighter the cold, slippery glass of milk. Her mouth dry, she took a quenching gulp, then hurriedly licked away the foolish milk mustache she felt painted across her upper lip.

Mack's eyes followed the movement.

The room got hotter.

Mack abruptly stood. "Afternoon break is over," he announced.

Humming another Sinatra tune, Ray led Kimmy away. The dogs followed, though Corndog threw Carly a last, friendly glance.

She tried not to smile at any of them.

Even with the room cleared out, the heat remained.

Mack didn't stop looking at her, but he gestured toward the door. "I have to be so careful. Because of Kimmy. All of them."

Carly nodded quickly. Somebody—Kimmy, herself—could be hurt by getting too attached. She was leaving town. He was a man with all the things she didn't want. The heat *had* to be ignored.

It was still there between them, though. When the man moved, even the stirred air brushed like a warm caress against her skin. Agreeing that it was dangerous couldn't make that kind of awareness disappear.

The truth of that was in Mack's face, too. He walked closer. "About that confession—"

"I have one myself." Carly tried desperately to think what it could be and why she suddenly needed to be the one to say the words that kept him away.

What could she say to cool the room, to break the shimmering tie between them? "This may make everything easier," she said.

He was so still she could see the pulse beating in his neck. Strong, tanned neck. *Thrum-thrum-thrum.* His pulse beat faster.

She briefly closed her eyes. Swallowed. Behind her back she crossed the fingers. "I don't like kids. Animals, either."

The room actually cooled. Immediately. Several degrees.

"I'm just not a kid and animal person." She said it louder, even with a little conviction. Man, she should've been knocking on doors in Hollywood. "So I have to be careful, too."

5

TGIS, Carly thought—Thank God it's Saturday—as she pushed her cart through the grocery store. She wore shorts and her running shoes because Varney's Marketplace was like everything else in Southern California—bigger than life. A woman got in a 5K walk going from extra-sharp cheddar to paper towels.

Sighing, she dug her list from her pocket. Even though she was moving in less than a month, she couldn't let her cupboards go completely bare. Toothpaste, coffee, fruit. Something to prepare in the evenings after a rough day at the home office.

Mack's home office.

After her little fib yesterday—that she wasn't a kid or animal person—the room's atmosphere had definitely eased. But still, she nearly skipped down his walkway at five o'clock. *Whee!* Two days Mack-free.

The fib still bothered her, but somehow it made the chemistry between them feel less dangerous to her. And heck, maybe it wasn't such a lie after all. Truly, she wasn't interested in *men* with kids and animals and Sinatra-fan fathers. She'd stumbled on that path before, skinning her knees and breaking—no, bruising—her heart.

A smart woman would revel in her single state and save all that breathless chemistry for the right kind of man. A smart woman would buy gooey ice cream, a bottle of expensive Chardonnay and a *Vogue* magazine then just enjoy the heck out of the weekend.

Whee, remember? Two days Mack-free.

She got in line with her meager load of nutrition and maxi-load of junk, gripping her determinedly cheerful mood with both hands. Even the fact that every checkout lane was as congested as the Ventura Freeway on Monday mornings wasn't going to bug her.

She relaxed her shoulders and rolled her neck, inspecting the lanes to her right. No, the long lines weren't going to bug her—but the sight of Mack and his daughter, Kimmy, standing in one, two lanes away, was going to do that all by itself.

She didn't want to see him. She absolutely didn't want him to see her. Not with wine and ice cream and unreduced-fat chips in her cart. The man would think she was a pig or a wino. Certainly lacking in some basic health smarts.

Five long strides to snatch up the biggest magazine on the racks lining the checkout lanes. A quick scuttle back, and she opened the thing at face level to feign an intense interest in Dolly Parton's recipe for alien-squash pie.

Something metallic gently bumped the back of her thigh. Someone short giggled. A familiar voice murmured in her ear. "Didn't take you for a fan of *The National Exposé.*"

A very inconvenient wash of goose bumps trailed

down her neck. *Great.* Now he'd think she couldn't control her hots for him.

She turned casually, calmly. Smiled. "Hey, I didn't know you shopped here."

Mack grinned. "We saw you from the line over there. Yours looked shorter. More interesting."

She ignored that, but couldn't ignore the tug on her T-shirt. "I'm Kimmy, remember?" The little girl wore a rose-printed party dress.

"Of course I do." Carly smiled at her politely, remembering her fib. She had to pretend disinterest. Had to pretend she didn't see that the bows tied in the girl's French braid were sloppy and that her lace-edged anklets weren't turned over properly.

Maybe it was something in the female makeup. Like some men she knew who cringed at a car idling roughly, her hands ached to touch the ribbons and socks. A tiny adjustment here, a minor redo there.

"Candy's birthday party is today," the little girl announced. "We're going to Toys 'R' Us next." She turned to her father, frowning. "I don't think I want to get her a Barbie."

Mack groaned. "I thought it was all settled. Do you have another idea?"

The ribbons unloosed a little more when Kimmy shook her head.

"C'mon, Kim." Mack sighed. "You know I'm lousy at this. Unless we're shopping for sports equipment or computer supplies, kiddo, it's up to you."

Kimmy bit her lip. "Um…"

Carly bit hers, too. She wanted to suggest a selection of hair scrunchies or those washable markers that stamped letters or cute little graphics. But that wouldn't go along with her disinterest in children.

"Maybe a baby doll," Kimmy said.

Dolly-Go-Lightly. Peter's daughter, Laurel, had craved one last Christmas, even though she thought she was almost too old for dolls. Carly had bought it for her and then dragged out her sewing machine and made a couple of outfits for the sweet-faced doll. She didn't know who had played with it more at Christmas, Laurel or herself.

"What are you smiling about?" Mack asked.

Carly started, then hurriedly pushed her cart forward. Wouldn't do to share that reminiscence. She cast about for another topic, glancing at his groceries. "Quite a haul."

He laughed. "Milk. Dog food. Cat food. Some more dog food."

"And Cheerios. You got 'em, right Dad?"

He tugged on Kimmy's braid. "Got 'em, kid. And we'll need to get 'em again—and everything else—in about five days."

Everything else included chicken and hamburger and lettuce, fresh fruit. Carly spied a six-pack of beer in there, too, so she relaxed a bit about her own bottle of wine. She sighed. In comparison to her basket of mood food and frozen lean entrées, his selection was downright wholesome. Domestic.

"Smiling," Mack said, "then sighing. What's up?"

She touched a frozen enchilada meal—280 calories—to let the cold burn bring her back to reality. "Just thinking about how hard it must be to keep up

with all those animals.'' Did that sound distant enough?
Disdainful even?

Mack shrugged. ''We love the critters.''

''So how come you didn't follow in your father's
footsteps? You didn't want to become a vet, too?''

He hesitated.

Kimmy grinned, and Carly itched again to fix the
limp ribbons and the askew socks. ''Granddad says
Daddy's squeamy—'' She looked up quickly at her father and corrected herself, ''squeam*ish*.''

Was that a red flush Carly saw creeping up Mack's
cheeks? ''So you don't like blood and guts, huh?''

Kimmy answered for him again. '''Fraid of them.''

Mack gave her braid another tug. ''I can do blood
and guts fine, just not on a daily basis.'' He tugged
lightly again. ''Hey, didn't I get you to the hospital,
cool as a cucumber when you split your chin? Who
held your hand when the doctor stitched you, huh?''

Carly's heart twisted but she refused to acknowledge
the small pain. So, a father shouldn't have to face his
daughter's injury alone. That didn't mean that *she*
should be the one wanting to hold *his* hand.

Kimmy leaned against her father. ''Thank you,
Daddy.'' She kissed his forearm.

Carly looked away from the tender moment. It made
her ache, it made her melty, it made her antsy. It made
her want to do *something*. ''Hey, Mack,'' she said,
thinking quickly. ''Could you grab me a bag of apples
from that bin over there?'' She pushed her cart forward
as if she was afraid to leave it alone. As if there still
weren't five people ahead of her in line.

Mack obligingly took the bait, and with his back

turned Carly grabbed the manufactured opportunity to ask Kimmy to turn around. "Just a quick fix to the bows," she whispered, and straightened the obviously man-tied ribbons. Then she knelt, and folded over the anklets so the right side of the lace showed and the embroidered rosettes faced out. "There."

Kimmy beamed. "Thanks," she whispered back.

The word went straight to Carly's stomach. She took in a long breath. Just like a rough idle, she reminded herself. I'm just predisposed to tying hair ribbons. She wasn't any more interested in Kimmy than she was interested in Kimmy's dad.

He plopped the bag of apples in her cart. Carly wasn't even particularly fond of apples, but she'd asked for them. She smiled.

He smiled back. Warmly. Male-ly. Deliciously.

Uh-oh. Carly's smile died as a nervous shiver traveled along her arms. She felt blindly for the frozen enchiladas.

Mack leaned closer.

The shivers tickled the back of her legs now. "What?" she asked hoarsely.

He glanced back at Kimmy, who was a few feet away inspecting a rack of kiddie toys. "I had an idea," he said.

She hoped it was nothing like the ideas she was having, because she didn't think she could say no for both of them. Swallowing, she stared into his eyes. Dark, like secret cravings. She swallowed again. "What's your idea?"

"You said you really didn't care for kids or animals.

So I thought I'd offer to work at your place if the atmosphere at mine bothers you.''

Bothers her? Carly tried to think clearly. At his house: Mack and pretending not to like the cute kid and the adorable animals. At her tiny condo: Mack and no distractions whatsoever.

Reprieve or disaster?

She stared at his mouth for some reason. She wasn't thinking about the nice shape or anything. Not for a second did she remember its warm hardness on her own.

Kimmy suddenly danced between them, her patent-leather Mary Jane shoes tapping against the linoleum floor. Behind her, in Mack's cart, was a big bag of dog food with a grinning canine on the package. He grinned like the yellow Lab, Corndog.

Mack would be the same tempting man no matter where they worked. But at his house were the added seductions of pets and charming relatives. There was only one answer.

''I'm fine at your house. No problem at all.'' That mouth of his curved up in another great smile. Under its warm power she barely remembered that wasn't the answer she'd intended to give.

Mack stood in the garage, spoiling for a fight, and the only available opponent was a chest-high stack of empty boxes. Muttering an oath, he thrust his fist at the cardboard, toppling the tower.

''Help any?'' His father came through the door leading to the backyard, carrying red-handled pruning shears.

"No, dammit." Frustrated anger throbbed dully in the pit of Mack's gut. "Kimmy woke up crying last night."

"Again?"

He pinched the bridge of his nose. "Yeah. Calling for her mother."

"No word from Suzanne lately, hmm?" Ray hung the shears on a nail above the workbench and pulled leather-palmed gloves from a drawer.

"Not even a postcard." Mack's ex worked for a cruise line and spent most of her time out of the country. "But when it's convenient, she'll show up and demand a visit. As usual." Another spurt of anger burned in his belly, and his hand again fisted.

"You're doing fine with Kimmy by yourself, son."

Mack gave his father a wry smile and forced his hand to relax. "Then why is she crying for her mother in her sleep?"

His father ignored the question. "Speaking of sleep, Mack, how much are you getting these days?"

"Let's just say I heard the Sunday paper hit the driveway at 5:00 a.m."

His father shook his head. "Ever since you started at Cycle, you've been restless. Are you sure it was right to take this job?"

Mack began to restack the boxes. "The job's fine, Dad." Wouldn't do to admit it wasn't the *work* that kept him awake nights.

"You need to have a little more fun."

"*Right.* I'll squeeze that into my agenda right between my responsibilities as Cycle's president and my obligations as Kimmy's father."

"President. Father. Don't forget you're still a man, Mack."

Carly popped into his mind. Wild curls, green eyes, a body that would wrap around him—

He shut out the image. "Don't worry, Dad. There's no danger of that."

"Still, you need to smell the roses. Enjoy yourself."

"Gotcha, Dad," Mack said absently, retrieving the last box. The tower stacked to Carly height.

"Kimmy's got that play date this afternoon. Why don't you take off and do something just for yourself?"

"Mmm." With his foot Mack tried sliding the cardboard column toward a corner of the garage.

"You could take those boxes over to Carly's. Didn't you tell me she's moving?"

Carly. Wild curls. Green eyes. A body that made him feel like...a man. His foot jerked. The tower toppled.

Damn, the boxes were an inconvenience. "Good idea, Dad."

It wasn't until Mack pulled into Carly's condo complex that he finally thought through what he was doing. How he'd been manipulated.

Damn conniving father. How had "something just for yourself" become "take those boxes over to Carly's"? And how had he been so stupid to fall for it?

The anger he'd felt that morning resurged as he gathered up an armful of flattened boxes. He didn't have time for this. He didn't have any business with Carly. No time for another woman on her way out of his life.

Getting involved with her would just be another responsibility.

Thank God he hadn't called her ahead of time. He would dump the cardboard on her doorstep and get the hell out.

Except she heard him when he got there. The boxes rasped against the screen door, and he saw her come toward the open entry wearing a short, loose dress.

Her mouth opened. "What—"

Across the concrete pathway to a neighboring condo came a loud shriek. Mack noted a bouquet of balloons tied on the neighbor's entry light.

Carly grimaced. "It's the weekend for birthday parties," she said over another chorus of squeals. "You better come in."

So he'd dump the boxes on her living room floor and then get the hell out of there.

Her perfume softened his brain. Sweet and elusive, he followed it inside and stood on the sky blue carpet, breathing it in.

Her eyebrows rose. "And you're here for—?"

"Boxes," he said tersely. "My dad suggested you might like these for your move."

He didn't point out that she could have brought them home herself the next day. She didn't point it out, either. Maybe she didn't think of it anymore than he had until this instant.

Damn perfume. Damn Carly.

"Well, uh, thanks." She gestured toward a corner of the room by a cream-colored love seat. "Maybe over there?"

He strode across the carpet, then leaned the flattened

stack against the sliding glass doors that led to a small patio.

"Nice place," he said. A small pond, complete with gurgling waterfall, bordered the patio. "You own it?" He glanced her way, suddenly noticing the way her hand was nervously combing through her curls. He wanted to touch them, too, to know if what looked like spun candy would feel as sweet against his palm.

As sweet as her mouth had tasted.

He made a move her way and she backed up a step. "No, and I'm lucky that the owner is letting me out of my lease agreement early."

She retreated again, looking at him as if he was the wolf ready to gobble up Goldilocks. *Hell*. It was Carly, her perfume, her lips, that were gobbling up his good intentions. Every one of his clear thoughts.

He wanted her and he couldn't have her, and it made him so damn mad.

Okay, an unreasonable emotion. To disguise it he turned away from her and took in the room, cool blue carpet, cool blue paint. An antique pine armoire against one wall, on the other, some shelving with a TV, stereo equipment and an aquarium.

A deep breath diluted the simmer in his belly. Her place was so different from his. No toys, no pet hair, no scrabbling claws against hardwood floors, no little-girl giggles. He didn't know what he thought of the quiet except that he didn't belong in it.

Good thing to remember.

He walked toward the shelves, gave a cursory inspection of her CD collection, then ran his fingers down the cool glass of the aquarium.

A fairly basic setup, with filter, heater, gravel. No water. No fish.

In the distance, through the screened front door, he heard a faint ''Daddy!'' His head instinctively lifted.

''The party,'' Carly said with a little smile. ''Somebody else's little girl.''

Somebody else's little girl. But he still had one himself. Who cried for Mommy in her sleep. A mommy who'd left her and Mack. Kimmy was sadder, but he was wiser.

He trailed his fingers over the aquarium again. ''You thinking about getting some pets, after all?''

She shifted her weight, her bare feet digging into the carpet. ''I had some tropical fish a while ago.''

''Yeah?''

''I, um, took them back.'' She looked away, out the patio doors toward that bubbling waterfall. ''They looked sick. They had these weird white spots on them.''

Little girls squealed in the distance again. It almost sounded like crying from here, like Kimmy's tears in the night. Mack's anger climbed out of his gut toward his heart.

''So you left them when the going got tough, huh?''

Her brows came together. ''Are you talking about the fish, Mack?''

''Whatever.'' He shrugged. ''Fish. Jobs.'' The burn was back. Carly, attractive, arousing, *leaving.*

Her eyebrows stayed a straight line. ''I am *not* running away from the job.'' Something hot was in her voice, too. Maybe they were both looking for a fight.

"So what are you running away from?" he asked.

"Me?" For God's sake what made him say that?

She crossed her arms over her chest, her eyes going from pale gray-green to green fire. "Don't think it's from you! I came to work the day we met with my resignation speech prepared and practiced."

"Yeah, but you couldn't be persuaded to stay when I needed you." Nothing he said was making the least logical sense but he couldn't keep quiet. "When *Cycle* needed you."

More irrational words shimmered between them. *I don't want to be attracted to you. It isn't making me happy either.*

Kid shrieking restarted, louder now, it floated around the room. Around them.

"Little girls make a lot of noise," Mack said.

"Yeah."

He hadn't forgotten she was no fan of kids. His temper heated again. "You can't take them back when they get sick."

"I know the difference between a fish and a child, Mack." Carly's bare toes tapped against the carpet. He tried not to stare at her pink-tipped feet. Tried to keep his gaze from traveling up to her bare legs.

Arousal and anger twined tightly.

"Why did you really come here?" she asked.

Believe it or not, he had an answer. And it spilled quickly, tersely, from between his gritted teeth. "Because you're inside my head," he said. "Because I wanted to remind myself why you shouldn't be."

She swallowed, and he followed the movement

down her pale neck. "I'm not responsible for you, Mack." Her voice was quiet.

It didn't calm him. "That's right. You don't want responsibility. You want it to be easy. No trouble. You want—"

"You have no idea what I want!" She took three angry steps toward him.

"Right again!" He met her with two steps of his own. "And I don't want to know! I don't want to know anything about you. I don't want to think about you or wonder how your hair can curl like this." He gathered a handful, pulling her face back for his gaze. "I don't want to lie awake at night wondering how many freckles you have and how long it would take me to count them."

His mouth came so close to her lips her breath washed his chin.

Silence grew like a bubble around them. Mack didn't think he'd ever heard such quiet. Certainly never since Kimmy had been born.

Kimmy.

"Go home to her, Mack." Carly's husky voice burst the intimate bubble. Had he whispered aloud his daughter's name?

"Go home to Kimmy and Corndog and Grits. All of them. All those that belong to you. Only to you."

Birthday party squeals and shouts clamored like good sense in his brain.

One by one his fingers released their hold on her hair. The strands tried grabbing back, curling around his knuckles even as he drew away.

6

—◆—

"I'm off then," Carly said, speaking softly in Mack's direction.

One hand still glueing the phone receiver to his ear, he used the other to wave her a casual salute.

Breathing a sigh of relief, Carly left the office, shutting the door—and Mack out of her life.

Another day without disaster. She allowed herself another sigh, not that it was all that necessary.

That ridiculous fight at her house a few days before had actually cleared the air, like a nice brisk wind blowing the smog out of the L.A. valleys.

Not that the awareness had gone away, but Mack's very open acknowledgment of it, and his annoyance with it, made the hours in the office easier to bear.

Before, they'd had to act normal, and react normally, when they made casual skin-to-skin contact or when their gazes happened to cross.

Now, they made darn sure not to touch each other at all. To avoid his eyes, she addressed his back, one of his shirt buttons, or sometimes even his gold pen. She had no idea where he looked when speaking to her. She kept her gaze on her work, or on the clock, so she could leave as promptly at five as possible.

Steps from the front door, the beguiling smell of bacon and sausage drifted from the large, blue-tiled kitchen. She could risk her usual stop to say goodbye to Ray, Kimmy and the animals. Mack was still safely ensconced in the office.

"Breakfast for dinner!" Kimmy announced from the kitchen table as Carly entered. "If I beat Granddad at Old Maid I'm crackin' the eggs."

The two cardplayers faced off across a scarred oak table. Ray held a fistful of cards, while Kimmy's were contained in a plastic holder that fanned them in front of her. Familiar with the late-afternoon ritual, Carly grabbed a soda from the refrigerator and dropped into another chair at the table.

With a clatter of dog tags, Cookies and Milk wandered over for a scratch. Corndog did his usual belly-flop onto her feet. Leaning out of her chair, Carly made a discreet peek toward the hallway. Mack had looked pretty busy, so if she kept this visit brief, she shouldn't blow her don't-like-kids-and-pets cover.

"I'm beatin' him, Carly," Kimmy said in a fierce whisper.

Carly nodded at the pile of pairs Kimmy had stacked in front of her. "I think she's got you again, Ray." She set down her sweating can to do her usual straightening of Kimmy's ribbons.

"I'm taking her to Vegas next," he said as Kimmy picked another card from his hand. She whooped as her choice made another pair for her stack.

Carly watched in silence for a few minutes. Sinatra sang in the background about love and marriage. For a moment it was almost too much. Warm breeze, warm animals, card games and sappy songs. Love and marriage. Gritting her teeth, Carly closed her eyes and overlaid the sentimental words with a vision of the "Married with Children" Bundy family.

Love and marriage probably *wasn't* all it was cracked up to be.

"I won! I won! Granddad got the Old Maid!"

Carly opened her eyes and smiled at Kimmy.

"You wanna play me next?" the little girl asked.

Yesterday Mack had gone out at five for a meeting with one of the Cycle product teams. Carly had stayed until past six playing Go Fish with Kimmy. It wasn't so safe today.

She shook her head, smiling. "Naw. Better not. Anyhow, I don't have to play Old Maid. I *am* an old maid."

Kimmy laughed with delight. Carly had made the word play a few days before, and once she'd explained it to the little girl, Kimmy had laughed with each repetition of the joke. Carly smiled again. Little kids were like that. Laurel had been the same way.

Sinatra started singing something else, and Kimmy swung toward her grandfather. "Gotta dance, Granddad. It's our dancing song."

This was familiar to Carly, too. She leaned back in her chair and sipped the cold soda, contentedly watching Kimmy do the fox-trot, her bare feet on top of Granddad Ray's shoes. Carly would just enjoy this one last thing before returning to her too-quiet and too-empty apartment.

The dancing couple halted in front of her. "Carly, next," Kimmy commanded.

She protested, but it was much too hard to resist the tug of Ray's hand and his charming smile so similar to Mack's. He moved her expertly, his bad knee apparently not a hindrance, pushing her in, then out, with the swinging beat. "Even old maids get a dance or two," Ray said.

She grinned. "An old maid will take a dance or two." With a quick movement she kicked off her shoes and twirled across the kitchen's hardwood floor.

"Don't know what's wrong with you young people," Ray admonished. "You and Mack both should be working less and dancing more."

Sinatra swung into "Chicago," and Carly tried following the lead of Ray's quick feet. "Dancing's pretty risky, Ray."

He frowned. "You sound too much like Mack." And as if one thought followed logically from the other, "You should stay for dinner."

He asked her every night. She smiled. "No, thanks." Same answer every night, too.

"Why not?" It was the first time he'd asked that.

She gave him an honest answer. "Because it's a family dinner. Your family. I don't belong here." And *I'll get hurt if I begin thinking I do.*

The song changed again. With a sudden sense of the time, Carly halted. She'd better leave before Mack emerged from the office.

"Don't stop on my account."

Too late.

She turned toward Mack and stared at the tanned vee of skin at the neck of his shirt. "I was just going."

Her gaze skittered away to search out her abandoned shoes.

Ray was back to fox-trotting with Kimmy. "I tried to get her to stay for dinner," the older man said. "And told her the two of you should be dancing more."

"Yeah, Daddy! Dance with Carly." Kimmy beamed as Ray shuffled her by.

Carly crept under the table to retrieve her shoe, barely avoiding a swipe of Corndog's tongue. When she emerged, Mack held her other shoe in his hand.

He drew it out of range as she reached for it. "Maybe they're right," he said. "Maybe we ought to dance a little more."

"I'm leaving." She said it as if her purse wasn't more than six feet away. As if she wouldn't have to dig for her car keys.

He tossed her shoe away as if he didn't believe a word she said. "Dancing's got to be better than you addressing my shirt buttons all day long."

Despite the serious threat to her sanity, a corner of her mouth kicked up. "You noticed that, huh?"

He took the shoe she held in her hand. Tossed it, too. "I noticed that. Huh."

Sinatra was really going for fans this time. A soft, warm beat. A nice and easy song. Oh, yeah, "Nice and Easy." It sounded safe and comfortable. Mack pulled her into his arms.

Her skin tried leaping closer—tingles crowding toward his touch. "Nice and easy," she whispered to herself.

They started moving. Mack wasn't as smooth a dancer as Ray, or maybe it was her.

"Relax," Mack said, a smile playing around his lips. "I'm not going to do anything."

But he *was* doing something. He was affecting the way her breath flowed into her lungs. Now it was catching somewhere in her throat, and she had to force it down, along with the delicious scent of Mack's aftershave. Under her palm his shoulder burned hot and strong. Her heart beat fast and crazy in her ears.

He tugged on a lock of her hair. She looked up into his face. Met his gaze. His mouth was moving. She thought he said "Relax" again, but with her heartbeat syncopating to Sinatra's beat, she couldn't be sure.

The tension couldn't find a way out of her body. She tried letting it out with her air, through her toes, even visualized all the nervous energy giving one more twist to the curls in her hair, but instead it just built inside of her.

Mack, maybe trying to help, maybe tired of dancing with a woman as taut as a broomstick, pulled her closer against him. Her cheek turned onto his chest. His heartbeat drummed against her skin. Hers was still faster.

She had to go home.

To the quiet apartment and the empty boxes she should be filling. She pushed away from the heat of his chest. Mack's strength came through her hands, adding a low, reverberating bass note to all the sounds she was feeling with her body.

Looking up at Mack to say goodbye, she saw his mouth move again first. But the trumpets were *wah-wah-wah-ing* and her heart was beating loudly, and her awareness of him was a noisy warning bell, so she just nodded at whatever he said.

His mouth moved again. They stopped dancing. Ray spun Kimmy over to the CD player and thumbed off the music. Mack took his hands away from Carly's body. Everyday sounds rushed back.

Ray looked at her, beamed. "So glad you agreed to stay for dinner."

Carly made her way to the kitchen, carrying a steaming platter of scrambled eggs.

"Sorry it's nothing fancy," Ray said, following her with a basket of warm biscuits and a pitcher of milk.

"Oh, this is just fine." Carly studiously kept her eyes away from Mack, now seating Kimmy in her chair. It didn't matter what the menu was. Trouble had already been served.

She stepped carefully over Corndog's tail, which just emerged from beneath the table, and set the eggs on a wooden trivet.

The only way to recoup from the disastrous dance was to make it through dinner without drawing too close to the family—without dislodging Mack's belief in her disinterest in kids and canines.

A purring beast inspected the inside of Carly's ankles and she let out an uncalculated little shriek.

"Grits." Mack called to the cat that had suddenly surprised her.

Kids, canines and *felines*.

"Grits," Mack said again.

The cat left off weaving between her legs to trot through the open door that led to a laundry room.

Carly whistled in admiration. "A trained cat?"

"Dumb luck," Ray corrected cheerfully. "Grits just happened to decide on a detour by his food bowl."

Mack smiled wryly. "It's the only kind of luck I've encountered lately, Dad."

The food platters passed quickly around the small table. Mack sat at one head while Kimmy played hostess at the other. Carly, seated on Mack's right, kept her eyes on her plate. Small servings and quick bites and she'd be safely away in no time.

"It's Kimmy that Mistress Fortune smiles on in this family," Ray said.

"Does that mean I beat you, Granddad?"

Carly stifled her laugh.

"That's what it means, bug," Mack answered. "You've been winning at Old Maid again?"

"And Go Fish, too," Kimmy said excitedly, her fork lifting to point in Carly's direction. "The other today, I mean yesterday—"

Carly hastily swallowed. "Speaking of yesterday—" she didn't dare let Kimmy spill about their round of cards "—exactly what is the date? Now that we're no longer in the offices, I have a hard time keeping track of time." Her foot jiggled nervously, encountering the warmth of Corndog's fur. Without thinking, she began stroking the dog with her bare toes.

"It's because it's almost summer," Ray said. "The days are so long they seem to go on forever."

"Maybe that's it," Carly agreed. Beneath the table, Corndog shifted, and Carly stretched her foot to continue petting him.

"What, the hours in the office aren't just flying by?" One of Mack's eyebrows quirked in a challenge.

"There's an understatement." Beneath the table, her foot moved nervously, but she kept her voice cool. Almost teasing. "Not that the company isn't top-notch, but it's pretty hard to concentrate with sunshine and a swimming pool just a long dive away."

"I didn't take you for the easily distracted type," Mack commented. He held her gaze with his eyes.

She tried ducking away from the connection. "Work usually keeps me focused. But this time—"

"That's the problem with you two," Ray interjected. "Too much talk about work and not enough play. Bring your swimsuit over tomorrow and go for a dip when you feel like it, Carly."

"Yeah," Mack repeated softly. "Go for a dip when you feel like it."

Carly's foot fluttered against Corndog, but she ignored Mack and turned to Ray. "You sound just like my mother. All work and no play and how I'm becoming dull, dull, dull."

"But she has a plan for all that, doesn't she, Carly?" Mack's voice edged down her spine again. "Something about marrying you off?"

Carly stilled. So he *had* heard that conversation with her mother. "You were listening."

He shrugged. "Accidentally."

Ray looked puzzled. "You're getting married, Carly?"

Mack dropped his fork to his plate. "Yeah, Carly. You getting married?"

"There's a man back in my hometown..." Her foot resumed its nervous stroking of the dog. How could she explain it to them? That marrying the minister was just a joke—and yet her secret wish as well. They had books on marrying millionaires, didn't they? Then why couldn't she apply herself to falling in love with a nice, uncomplicated man?

"Getting married?" Kimmy piped up. "Who you marrying, Carly?" Her brown eyes sparkled with interest.

Ray's expectant face waited for an answer, too.

Mack's eyes took on an unholy glitter. She swallowed. "Well, someday...maybe in Indiana..."

"What's Indiana got over California?"

In response to Mack, Carly bit her lip. His jaw hardened. How could she explain her recent disappointment and the loneliness? This warm family wouldn't understand.

"Tell us about your wedding dress," Kimmy said. "I know it'll be *george*-ous."

Carly licked her lips. Deflect the conversation. Think of something else to talk about.

Mack's implacable expression gave no help at all.

"So you're really getting married?" Ray asked.

"Tell us. Tell us about the dress," Kimmy urged.

Carly cleared her throat. Searched desperately for something else to talk about. Could only concentrate on the hot glitter in Mack's eyes. "Maybe we should talk about the rowing machine project, Mack. Or the itinerary of our sales trip."

Ray groaned.

"I wanna hear about your wedding," Kimmy complained.

Mack offered no help at all.

"The stack of correspondence—"

Kimmy made a little-girl groan like her Granddad's. "The wedding, Carly."

Desperate, Carly could think of only one way to throw Kimmy off the scent. "Tell about our card game instead, Kimmy. How you beat me at fourteen straight hands of Go Fish."

Carly noted Mack's blink of surprise. With relief, she also noted that Kimmy gobbled the bait and recited a long-winded, card-by-card description of yesterday's wins. Then the little girl went on to tell about the Chutes and Ladders round they'd snuck in the day before that.

Not wanting to witness Mack's expression, Carly applied herself to her plate and took out all her fidgets on Corndog's warm coat.

Thankfully, the conversation moved on to a debate between Kimmy and Ray about the possible whereabouts of The President, the snake. She'd made it.

Suddenly a steely grip on Carly's thigh stilled the restless movements of her leg. Her head jerked up to meet Mack's gaze. "I don't understand you, woman," he said in an undertone.

The skin of her leg prickled beneath his touch. "What? So I played a few games with Kimmy. What's the big deal?"

He squeezed and the prickles raced toward the juncture of her thighs. "Pretty strange for a woman who doesn't like kids."

She shrugged, trying to ignore the heat warming her womb.

"And you still don't like animals, I presume."

She shrugged again.

He leaned closer, so close she could see the burning lights in the darkness of his eyes. "But I'm guessing you were petting the dog underneath the table."

"Why is that?" she asked faintly.

"Because I'm guessing you didn't mean to be running your nervous little toes up and down *my* leg."

For the first time in—forever—Mack knocked off work shortly after Carly left at five o'clock.

She wasn't hanging out in the kitchen. "Hasn't stayed since last week," his father commented without looking up from his hand of cards.

"She doesn't want to play anymore, Daddy," Kimmy said. "Why not?"

Why not? The *why not* was as fascinating as the *why* she had played games with Kimmy in the first place.

The *why* she'd been stroking the dog under the table that night was as fascinating as why wouldn't she discuss her impending marriage plans or anything else remotely personal.

He'd been trying for just that information since last week.

"She said she was going to the mall," his father said casually.

"Yeah?" He shoved his hands in his jeans and tried not to calculate how much a head start she had on him.

"You need some time away from the office, son," his father said, this time looking him in the eye. "And since home is office, why don't you take off for a few hours? Go get yourself something to eat."

He caught his father's drift this time. Denied the thought about his desire to follow Carly and instead thought about sitting down with his father and his daughter and his pets. Playing a game of cards.

Or if he couldn't sit still, conduct an all-out search for The President.

But something about Carly made him feel more than son, father, pet keeper.

He grabbed up his keys, gave a quick kiss to Kimmy and let himself out of the house.

The shopping center was small, shaded by date palms, and quiet in the after-work hour. Because it was Friday, everyone must be at happy hour or a pizza place with their kids. Mack didn't have a clue where to find Carly, he only knew that he would.

If she hadn't said she didn't like kids or pets. If she hadn't then become Kimmy's latest victim and Corndog's latest idol, maybe then he couldn't have this unreasoning need to find out *why* and *why not.*

He thought he saw the hem of her yellow skirt flutter into the bookstore up ahead.

Fifteen aisles and one surprised grandmother later, he discovered he was wrong.

Department store? Shoe store? Ice cream shop?

He strode past the pet store, only catching a glimpse of Carly at the very last moment. At the back of the empty shop, she knelt. Tanks of tropical fish lined the walls, and the glow of the aquarium light washed over her face. She had one hand pressed against the glass. Visiting the fish she'd returned?

After a few minutes she pushed open the door to leave. The bells on the door jangled, and the paper bag in her hand rattled as she slipped out. She only noticed him when he blocked her turn toward the parking lot.

In the late afternoon the sunshine washed the gray out of her eyes. Pale green, like water of a clear creek, they met his directly for the first time in days.

"What are you doing here? Did I forget something? Do you need something?"

Answers. The touch of her skin. The taste of her mouth. "What are you shopping for?" he said instead.

She threw a swift, backward glance through the pet store windows. "Stuff."

He looked at the bag in her hand and read from its design. "'Winter's Store for Girls'?"

She shrugged. "A birthday present for someone I know."

A present. Something for another child. "Where are you going now?"

"Did you need something?" she asked again.

He put his hand beneath her elbow. "Where are you going now?"

She stepped away from his touch. "Home."

He followed her as she hurried off in the direction of the parking structure. She frowned at him. "If you don't need something from me, I'm perfectly capable of getting to my car."

After more than eight torturous hours alone with her in his office, it seemed odd to him, too, that he still wanted to be with her. "I'll just make sure, if you don't mind."

Maybe she did mind, but with a sigh she continued on her way. He hoped by the time they reached her sedan that he'd have it all figured out—what he wanted to ask her, what he wanted from her.

At her car, deep in the structure's depths, she dug

out her keys, then climbed inside. Obviously thinking twice about it, she unrolled her window and stared up at him. "Can I give you a ride to your car or something?"

He didn't wait for a second invitation, sliding into the passenger seat quickly. With one more glance at him, she lifted her hand to insert the key.

He caught her fingers in his. "You're a fraud, I've figured that out, you know. I just can't figure out why."

7

He couldn't see her expression in the cool, dark interior of the car. And though beneath his fingers her hand trembled, her skin itself burned his flesh.

"Why did you follow me?" Her voice sounded burned, too, raw and dry.

Why. "Because there's something between us besides claims of disinterest and stabs at denial." He took a breath. "That damn kiss."

Despite what she'd said, Carly had entertained his daughter and charmed his father and pleased his pets. Despite all her protests and all his wariness he wanted to kiss her again.

Why not.

He cradled her cheek in his palm.

"Mack…"

He flexed his fingers, pressing lightly into her flesh, to let her know he wasn't going to let her go. "Not this time," he said.

"Maybe…maybe we'll be disappointed."

He laughed.

"Okay, then perhaps that's the reason we shouldn't."

Something quiet and painful in her voice stilled him.

"That's why you lied? Because our one kiss was too—undisappointing?"

"I wouldn't say I lied."

"You claimed you didn't like animals. Kids, too."

Her breath blew across his wrist. "Just for the sake of argument, let's say I did...prevaricate." She pushed his hand away from her face. "Wouldn't I have a darn good reason?"

He'd gotten nowhere figuring it out. "Just for the sake of argument, what could it be?"

"I'm leaving in a month."

"There's that."

"We work together."

"Right." But he didn't believe either of those—or both—was the answer.

"And..." Her hand rose in a helpless gesture.

He grabbed hold of it to entwine their fingers. Smooth and hot, her skin slid against his. A quivering burn zipped up his arm. In the darkness her breath hitched.

"Carly," he whispered hoarsely. He couldn't think of *why* any longer, only *why not*.

Despite all his worries about involvement, he was hungry for her. The sound of her shallow breaths made his heart pound.

Why not.

He sifted the fingers of his free hand into her spun-candy hair, then brought a handful of it to his face, rubbing it against his mouth.

She made a quick, stifled sound, and the smell of her perfume rose like heat into the air.

His pulse jumped a gear higher, but her sounds, her

fragrance, the almost weightless touch of her curls against his face was just too good to rush. He brushed the sweet stuff against his cheeks, feeling its slight catch against his afternoon beard.

She made the sound again. "Mack," she said, leaning forward.

And she kissed him.

She kissed him as if she was saying it was over, and that was what she probably intended. She pressed her warm—so warm—lips against his mouth, pressed gently like she was saying good-night to a first date or goodbye to a casual friend. When it was over—very, very quickly—he laughed because he wasn't going to let her off so easily.

"Honey," he said, stroking her face with his thumb. "You must have been kissing some namby-pamby men."

"Mack." She groaned. "For gosh sake, we both know this isn't a good idea."

He traced her skin from temple to chin. "And later we're going to talk about why that is."

Her breath shuddered into her lungs; he felt it tremble through her body, causing his heat and hardness to press tighter against his jeans. "But that's later. Right now I want to taste you."

And he bent his head for her kiss.

So much for her protests. Her lips, smooth as a baby's skin, didn't back away from his. At the first pressure she made a little sound—a cat's contented purr—and it traveled through him, hardening his body, dizzying his mind.

This was his chance. *Break through to her.* His

tongue tickled the seam of her lips, and she gave up her last defense, her body surging toward him, her mouth opening. Their tongues touched, their shoulders bumped and the sweet wetness of her mouth made him forget all sense of time and place.

He broke away from her mouth to drag in a breath, and then he succumbed to his hunger for her again. He softly bit her cheek, the clean line of her jaw. The pulse at her neck tasted wild and ready for him.

She moaned as he pulled the silk T-shirt from the waistband of her slim skirt. Her goose bumps rose to meet the sensitive tips of his fingers as he traced blindly over her ribs to her bra. His pounding heart urged his mouth back to her lips, and at the same moment that his tongue stroked hers, his thumb stroked the tip of her breast.

Mouth wet and soft. Nipple hot and hard.

"Carly."

Her body trembling, she pressed into his hand. Desire shot through him, impossibly tightening him. He stroked into her mouth again, closed his other hand over her other breast. Her fingers tangled in his hair.

Her touch and taste transported him again. He was not father or business executive any longer. He was a man, holding a woman's soft flesh in his hands, holding her incredible femaleness. His body was twenty again, eighteen. His attitude changed, too. All his cynicism and disappointment were burned clean away by her sweet passion.

A beach-baby song. A taste of female new and true. The front clasp of her bra yielded to his determined fingers. He pushed the warm fabric aside to take her even warmer breasts into his mouth.

He groaned. *Carly.*

So new, so beautiful, so his.

He ran his thumbs over her wet nipples, the erotic sensation clawing at his body. He still couldn't read her expression in the darkness, but her hands slid from his hair to trail down his chest.

Her fingers crawled beneath his shirt, and his flesh shuddered as she found his naked skin. He took her mouth again, penetrating it, searching for everything about her he could have. Everything she'd offer up to him.

He shuddered again, groaned as he shifted closer. He *needed* to be closer to Carly.

Suddenly he was sixteen again, too frustrated to figure out a way to touch all a woman's softness in the close confines of a heated car. He drew away from her mouth to rest his forehead against hers.

Their heavy breaths only jacked his desire higher. "Honey, honey. We've got to find a better place than this car."

Her eyes closed, he could see that much, and she tried to inch away from his hands.

He released her breasts, but held her lightly around the rib cage, unwilling to let her get away. Her fingers drifted off his flesh.

He groaned. "Carly, honey. Don't give up on me now."

But she pulled back from his touch, completely disengaging them. With a quick gesture she yanked down her top and crossed her arms over her breasts. "This

is exactly the problem," she said tightly. "Exactly why
I told you I don't like kids and animals."

Why? He tried to focus on what she was saying instead of the unsteady sound of her breaths and the pulsing beat of his blood. "What do you mean, honey?"

"I'm twenty-six years old! And I'm making teenage
love in the front seat of a car in a mall shopping center!"

He laughed hoarsely. "The same thing went through
my head. That's why I suggest we, uh, go someplace
else."

"You don't get it." She had that dense-male-alert
note in her voice.

He didn't live with a four-year-old daughter for
nothing. "Explain it to me, honey. God knows I'm
dumb as a post right now." He ran a finger down her
cheek. "Desire will do that to me."

She trembled, moved toward him, then retreated.
"*No.* That's the problem. You make me forget, too."

He touched her hair again, the will-o'-the-wisp stuff
tickling his palm. "Forget what?"

"I've been here before, Mack. And I promised myself I never would be here again."

He tried smiling. "Nearly making love in the front
seat of a car, honey? I had my own back seat experi-
ences, I promise you."

She made a little sound. Like his joking was hurting
instead of helping.

"Mack. There was another man not all that long ago.
He broke my heart, okay? And I haven't patched together the fickle thing just so you can do it all over
again."

Another man. A broken heart.

Two aisles away, a car vroomed to life. Headlights switched on. In the meager light it threw their way something glittered on Carly's cheek.

One tear. Hot and fat. He caught it with his thumb and brought it to his mouth to taste her distress.

She made another small sound. "That's why I said what I did, Mack. Why I've tried to stay away from you. Because if I get too close I forget all my promises and all my pain."

All my promises and all my pain. Hadn't he made them, hadn't he felt that, too?

The *why* and the *why not.*

Mack smiled grimly. Sixteen, eighteen, twenty, sped by, re-aging him in an instant. He was thirty-two again. A man with an arthritic, bitter heart.

This wasn't working. Carly rolled down her window, willing in fresh air, willing a new plan to breeze through.

Because all her earlier resolves and half-truths were busts. They hadn't bought her safety—instead they'd brought her to this moment.

His mouth on her. A hot, demanding mouth that she wanted to surrender to. To feel forever against her.

She half turned away from Mack to quickly reclasp her bra and smooth her shirt. She straightened one cramped leg, and her shoe bumped against her keys, fallen to the floor of the car.

Reaching for them, she turned her head Mack's way to avoid hitting the steering wheel. Her line of sight found his hands, his lean, long fingers. One was splayed against his thigh, the other made a tight, controlled fist.

One hand relaxed, one relentless.

Desire, caution.

Male, female.

Contradictions they couldn't resolve in the heated car with the memories of passion between them.

She cleared her throat. "What do you think we should do?" She tried swallowing away her hoarseness. "Maybe we can shuffle the product teams a bit. Find someone else to pair you with."

He was already shaking his head. "I don't want to mess with what's working."

Her keys bit into her palm. "*We're* not working, Mack."

His silence didn't sound like disagreement.

"Let me take you to dinner, Carly," he suddenly said, putting up a hand to stall her immediate protest. "Talk to me. Tell me about you. Then I think we can get past this."

What could she say? Pretty embarrassing to admit she hadn't a prayer of getting past her passion for him. If he thought he could do it, shouldn't she at least attempt the feat?

"Mack—"

"Carly."

He sounded so sure. She sighed. *Okay, fine.* She sighed again, then tried for humor. "You paying?"

He nodded.

"Then it's gonna cost you."

Across the parking lot of the shopping center was a favorite of Carly's, Chez Mexique, a restaurant featuring French-Mexican cuisine. "Don't ask," she cautioned Mack when he raised his eyebrows as they studied the menu. "Just eat."

Seated across a small, intimate table from Mack, even the delicate spiciness of the signature Chez Mexique appetizers couldn't burn the taste of him off her tongue. Her fingers closed tightly on her glass of *fumé blanc* and she stared down at the creases in the crisp tablecloth.

She *had* to cool the passion. Had to be sure he understood it couldn't be.

Over Mack's shoulder the maître d' seated a much younger couple at the table behind them. Chez Mexique was as casual as it was pricey, but the young man—late teens—wore a tightly knotted tie. Even on the warm summer evening his date had on stockings and high heels.

Their smiles were small and tight, but something surrounded the two of them besides nervousness. Excitement, urgency, a newness that made Carly smile.

"What are you thinking about?" Mack asked.

She shrugged, not wanting to explain. "Just... remembering." But had she ever experienced that with some young man? What she'd felt in the past seemed pale against the compelling need Mack built in her.

His touch cooled her cheek. "You're blushing. Must be some memory."

She jerked back from his fingertips. Couldn't go there. Didn't dare surrender again to that delight. "So what did you want to talk about?" she said, easing her chair a little farther from the table. Out of his reach.

"You. That you've been hurt before."

"Who hasn't?" She lifted one shoulder. "You get to a certain age, to a certain place in your life, and you're bound to have encountered heartache."

"Enough to make you run from passion?"

How could he say such a thing, so seriously? He didn't stammer or look away. His eyes stared into hers, forcing her to meet his challenge.

She swallowed a gulp of her wine. "*Passion*...is such a loaded word."

"What do you want to call it, honey? What we had in your car. What we *made* in your car."

Damn him. Heat traveled up her neck again, singeing the tips of her ears. She remembered his mouth, hard and blazing. On her lips. On her breasts.

He softly groaned. "God, Carly, don't look like that."

"Like what?" she croaked.

"Your eyes go green, you know. All the gray slips away and they burn." He took a breath. "They burn *me*."

A man shouldn't talk like this, she thought. Certainly Peter never had. She tried to think of the other men she'd dated, her boyfriend during junior year in college. Nobody had ever talked to Carly in words that made her flesh quiver and her nipples harden.

She closed her eyes. Opened them to refocus on the couple over Mack's shoulder. The boy carried the girl's hand to his mouth and laid his lips upon her palm.

Carly hastily redirected her gaze. "Let's talk about something else."

"Who hurt you, Carly?"

Just tell him. Give him all the details, outline all the

points of her pain, loneliness, disappointment. "Peter. His name was—is Peter."

"And?"

"And—" And what? What had Peter done to her, exactly? "We dated for about eighteen months. He'd been divorced for a couple years before we met. Peter's a real workaholic, which I think was what killed his marriage in the first place."

"But he found time for you." Mack said it like it was a certainty.

She frowned. "Well, some time. I was the lead on a big project most of those months, and I was working terrible hours, too." She'd made time for Laurel, though.

"The relationship sounds like it was…convenient."

She shot an assessing look at his neutral expression. "What are you getting at with that comment?"

His eyebrows rose at her defensive tone. "Two busy working people. *Healthy, normal,* working people. You know."

"Are you talking about sex?" she demanded. "I didn't date some man for 'healthy' and 'normal' reasons!"

"Shh, shh." Mack started laughing and at the same time reached out to grab her hand. "People are staring at us."

Her skin nearly sparked at his touch, and she drew her fingers away to tuck them safely in her lap. "Just so you understand," she said grumpily.

"I'm trying to." Something shone from his eyes besides leftover amusement. Relief, maybe?

She didn't try puzzling it out. "So there's Peter and me. You got that?"

He nodded.

"We suited each other. We...were kind to each other." And she'd loved Laurel. But that feeling was still too private to share with Mack. "We started talking about getting married."

"Convenience again," Mack said.

She nodded absently, remembering her eagerness to have a ready-made family. "It sounded good to me."

The young couple had been served drinks as they studied the menu. Colas. Carly barely remembered being that age. Ever feeling as happy as the boy and girl looked.

"What did you want when you were young, Mack? A career? A family?" How had she viewed her future at nineteen?

"Young? How young?"

She made a gesture. "I don't know. Late teens. Early twenties. Do you remember what you wanted?" She heard the wistful note in her voice. "What consumed your thoughts?"

"Honey, honey, honey." He shook his head in good-humored despair. "You really don't know the male animal at all, do you?"

"What?"

"At nineteen, twenty? What I wanted? What consumed me?" A wicked grin broke over his face. "Getting laid."

"Oh, you!" She slapped at him with her napkin, but he caught it deftly, then worked his fingers up the cloth toward her hand.

Carly's heart stuttered. She watched his advancing fingers in slow motion. All she had to do was let go.

She didn't, and his hot, lean, *knowing* hand encircled her wrist.

"What happened next, Carly?" His grin died and his grasp tightened. "You and Peter were talking about marriage. Then what?"

Could he feel the speeding beat of her pulse? Would he know that his touch set her blood on fire and that her heart pounded wildly to put out the flames?

She tried focusing on the past. "I don't really know what happened next. Maybe talking about marriage made Peter rethink his first one. A month after he brought up the subject he came over one night and told me he was remarrying his first wife."

Mack's fingers squeezed her wrist. "Bastard."

Without thinking, she put her free hand over the one Mack had touching her. "Don't say that. He was—is a nice guy."

"A workaholic who found a convenient female workaholic to pass a little time with."

"It wasn't like what you're thinking." So much of those months had been enjoyable times that included Laurel. She wished Peter and his family every happiness.

"Don't tell me what he was like. I can read between the lines if you can't, honey. He wanted a bed mate who was as busy with work as he was."

Carly didn't know whether to be offended or amused. "How can you be so sure, Mack?"

In anger, his eyes shadowed to near-black. The light from the rustic lantern on their table glittered in the darkness of his gaze. "I've been around you, Carly."

"So you assume he wanted a bed mate because that's what you want, huh?"

He didn't answer. Behind him the young couple exchanged a brief kiss. Carly recognized what shimmered off them now, and it was love. The sweet freshness of it made her ache.

Her fingers untangled from Mack's. "Taking the fifth, hmm? Because Peter wasn't out for sex, you know. As a matter of fact, we never once shared a bed."

Still trying to make sense of Carly's revelations, Mack watched her taillights recede in the distance. What an evening. What a meal. He'd found it difficult to eat with his jaw scraping the table. But he'd managed.

He'd ordered an entrée that was a cross between a crepe and a burrito. Though the idea seemed almost dangerous, the taste had been out of this world.

Like Carly. Dangerous, delicious.

But brokenhearted? By a man she'd never slept with?

His jaw was going slack again. He could feel it. And along with that flashed a burst of anger. Anger at Carly? At this Peter?

Who the hell knew or cared. The only certain thing was that he needed to set her straight.

Diving in his pockets for his keys, he jogged in the direction of his own sedan. Carly's relationship with Peter—her *nonsexual* relationship—wasn't the stuff of broken hearts.

She wasn't coming clean to herself or she wasn't coming clean to him.

Either way, their business remained unfinished.

8

The night was warm enough that Carly must have decided to leave the screen door latched across her front entry. Anger ignited Mack's blood again. A single woman should be more careful.

A man with no good on his mind might just decide to stop by.

He hesitated on her doorstep. Did that describe him—a man up to no good?

Maybe he should go. Leave her view of her past and her past men alone.

Through the screen came the click and beep of an answering machine. Carly must have pressed the button to play her calls.

He stepped back to the shadowed walk, but before he could retreat came the voice of Carly's mother. "It's about the minister, dear."

For the second time he found his feet rooted to the ground. Something about the woman's voice froze his ankles.

"About Matthew," she continued.

Matthew.

"I wanted to tell you how much he likes my cooking." She laughed a bit. "There was a potluck social in the church hall tonight. I brought a macaroni-and-cheese casserole and my snickerdoodles—you know everybody loves my cookies. But Matthew, he was particularly complimentary.

"Sweetie, he's going to make you a wonderful husband." Her voice sounded full of warmth, but almost teary.

Probably imagining giving her beloved daughter away to the guy.

"So there you are. Call me when you have a minute. I just wanted you to know again there's a good man in your future." *Click. Beep.*

Click. Beep. Mack's signal to leave.

To leave Carly and her past alone. But he raised his fist and rapped on the metal frame of her screen door instead.

It was Carly's future and her future man that he couldn't let go.

Since arriving home from Chez Mexique, Carly had quickly stripped out of her skirt and shirt to wash her face and brush her teeth. Her favorite keep-her-bangs-back hairband, black with white polka dots and circa seventh grade, was still circling her head when the metallic knock sounded on her front screen.

Guessing her neighbor Carol was at the door, Carly wandered as she was—headband, men's extra-small flannel boxers and a long T-shirt—toward her entry.

"Honey? Sugar?" Carly called out. "At this time of night you're always after something sweet."

"Is that right?"

Mack's deep voice made her jump. With her heart

pinballing against her insides, Carly took a couple more steps toward the door. "What are you doing here?"

The interior light was dim, and she didn't get too close to the screen, but his gaze touched her like hot fingertips. Neck starting to burn, she stripped away her ugly, stretchy hairband, tossing it toward the love seat.

"What are you doing here?" she asked again.

"Maybe I want that something sweet you're offering." His voice sounded determined, a little mad maybe. "Let me in."

The command dragged Carly another step forward. Then she stopped. "Wait a minute. Just tell me what you want first."

"Who are you expecting?"

Carly blinked. "Expecting?" She looked down at her home-alone outfit. "What makes you think I'm expecting anyone?"

He rattled the handle of the screen door. "Let me in."

The heat from his eyes, from the anxious burn on her neck entered her blood. Like a match to gasoline, flames raced along her nerves. She took another step closer.

The screen didn't blur the hard lines of his face. He rattled the door handle again, commandingly.

Carly's hand fingered the screen lock, then she thought better of it. "You still haven't told me what you want."

"You still haven't told me who you were offering yourself to."

She shook her head. "*What* are you talking about?"

"'Honey? Sugar?'"

She shook her head again. "I thought you were my neighbor. I wasn't offering *myself.* I was offering the real stuff."

"Same thing, sweetheart." His strong, wide palm flattened against the screen.

Like a finger running through hot bathwater, ripples of heated sensation rolled down Carly's spine. She met his dark, unreadable gaze.

"Let me in," he demanded.

She reached for the lock again, stopped herself. Instead, she trailed her fingernail across the screen, across the male palm still pressed against her doorway.

"Carly." Command? Warning?

"Tell my why you're here, Mack. Didn't we already say everything?"

"Maybe." He made an angry gesture. "No."

Hadn't she explained she refused to risk her heart again? After telling him about Peter, Mack had seemed quiet, subdued even. But now some emotion shimmered from him—sultry, smoldering, like steam. She was afraid to get closer to it.

"And for God's sake," he said. "You should lock your door at night."

"It's hot." Behind her the phone began to ring. She glanced over her shoulder.

"Let me in, Carly."

With the phone still distracting her, she hesitated.

"Now, Carly."

Feeling silly trading quips through the screen and wanting to make a dash for the phone, Carly quickly untwisted the lock and spun to head for the receiver.

Mack's hand encircled her upper arm. "Let the machine pick it up." His gentle, but intractable, grip made it impossible for her to pull away. "Probably your mother wanting to extoll the virtues of the saintly minister again."

"You heard that?" She tried tugging her arm away. "That was a private call."

He shrugged.

The phone stopped ringing but he didn't release her arm. Carly's breath rushed out unevenly. His mood made her nervous. She'd seen him laughing, businesslike, tender with his daughter, sexy as heck with her. But she'd never seen him like this.

"Maybe you should go," she said. How could her upper arm have a heartbeat? But where he touched her, her skin pulsed, sending sluggish waves of weakness toward her knees.

"Maybe not," he said.

The answering machine clicked. Her mother's voice entered the room. "Just wanted to tell you one more thing about Matthew," she said. "There was music at the social tonight…and dancing." An audible sigh. "It must be that military training. He's wonderful on his feet." Another click. A beep. A whir.

Mack's grip on her arm squeezed just the smallest bit. Carly stared at her toes and tried smiling. "Only my mother would think boot camp could improve one's fox-trot."

Mack didn't laugh. He didn't even smile back. His free hand grasped her chin and tilted it toward his face. "For God's sake, Carly, is that what you're looking for? A dancing master?"

Like heat lightning, an image of the two of them dancing in his kitchen flashed through her mind. She shivered.

As if he read her thoughts, as if her shiver was some kind of invitation—and maybe it was—he bent his head and took her mouth in a hot, angry kiss.

Oh, no. She should never have opened the door. She should really make him go. But her arms, the one having been suddenly released, wound around his neck.

They weren't far from the entry. As his head moved to angle the kiss, his foot reached out to catch the heavy front door and kick it closed. The lock snicked as it found its snug fit.

His mouth trailed across her cheek, breathed into her ear. "Let me in," he whispered.

Let him in? A rush of goose bumps prickled down her neck to her breasts. Her nipples rose tightly against the soft fabric of her T-shirt. If she let him into her body it would be too easy to let him into her heart. Oh, boy, it would be too dangerous.

He sucked on her earlobe, and her nipples began to ache sweetly. She pressed them against his chest, and he hauled her closer, his fingers splayed wide and firm on her backside.

His arousal pressed against her belly, an invitation, a demand, a test.

His lips moved across her face, sucked teasingly, too briefly, on her lower lip to find her other ear. "Let me in," he said again, his breath hot. "Let me in."

She couldn't let him in. No way could she take such a risk. Any minute now she'd push him away. Show him out the door.

The tip of his tongue traced her ear and she closed her eyes. She was so tired of pushing him away. He licked the sensitive skin of her temple. She was so tired of pretending this didn't feel extraordinarily good.

Maybe they could meet someplace else. Find passion and release somewhere outside of her heart.

Her hands tangled in his hair. He lifted his head, and she traced the hard plane of his face with her palm. Her thumb traced his lips, and he ducked his head to suck it into his mouth.

She thought she'd faint.

"Just this." She struggled to get the words out between the all-consuming, rapid beats of her heart. "No past, no future. No promises, no pain."

He gently bit the fleshy pad of her thumb. Overloaded with sensation, she pulled it out, rubbed it wetly against his mouth. "You understand? I'm not letting you in, Mack." Did he see what she wanted? "Just...take me someplace else." Would he know what that meant?

His mouth hovered over hers, dazzling her with want. "I get it, sweetheart," he said. "No pain, no promises." He looked deeply into her eyes, and she tried putting her needs there, her allowances and her restrictions. "And I have just the place to go."

Twining their fingers, he led her toward the bedroom.

Mack gripped Carly's hand tightly. He was way past conversation. Using the fragrance of her perfume as his guide, he strode toward Carly's bedroom.

So he didn't want the added burden of a relationship. Carly wasn't asking for that. She seemed to explicitly not want that. And want was the issue here. While taking Carly to bed didn't mesh with any of his roles—father, businessman, *et al.*—it was something he, Mack, the person, the *man,* wanted. Something just for himself.

Damn, he needed that. *Needed her.*

In the doorway he paused, drawing her back against his chest so he could hold her and soak up the look of her room at the same time.

Her exuberant curls tickled his chin and were mirrored in the frothy, frilly curtains at her window. Dim light from a Tiffany-shaded bedside lamp warmed peach walls. A lush fern hung by the window, fresh flowers in a crystal vase scattered petals over the antique dresser.

And he saw Carly, saw her truly, deeply. The romantic room held so many clues to the woman. Told him about all the ways he could please her tonight. Would please her.

Finally, he let his gaze wander to her bed. White again, lacy again. Pillows tumbled over it, fussy and sweet, and the thought of her laid out across the fussiness, stripped to the flesh and his touch, drew him up so hard and tight that he lost his breath.

Damn. Carly on that bed, naked and wanting him was an image as sensual as cool vanilla ice cream drenched in hot, sticky caramel.

He shuddered and, driven to tasting her, drew that candy floss hair away to suck the flesh of her neck. She moaned and reached behind them to grab his hips.

Sweet, sweet heat.

His arousal pressed into the small of her back, trying

to find its way to her. His fingers, finely trembling, drifted off her shoulders, slowly, gently, to lightly cover her breasts.

She surged against his hands, and his arousal surged, as well. *"Carly."* She moaned, and he echoed the sound as the hard buds of her nipples pressed against the centers of his palms.

Excitement burned deep in his belly, and he pushed himself against her again, searching for ease.

He backed off, took a breath. Just seconds ago he'd been planning a sweet seduction, thinking of all the ways he could please her, but with a movement, a sound and a response, she made him high-school-horny again.

Reluctantly, to regain control of himself, he brought his hands away from her breasts to her hips, kissed her temple gently. He heard disappointment in her sigh.

He laughed softly against the tickle of her hair. "We'll get there, sweetheart. I promise to let you have it all. It's just…just that you make me so damn *hot*." He turned her so he could see her face.

The warm desire in her eyes made him rock against her again. "See that?" he said. "I've got to slow down a bit."

She pushed forward with her hips, her legs shifting to make a place for him. "But I ache, Mack."

He closed his eyes and ran his hands down her back, holding her buttocks to push her against him. Fire seared from his groin, ran up his arms, down to his hands. His palms heated against the flannel of her shorts, and he thrust his hands beneath the fabric to find bare, warm flesh.

They shuddered together. "Mack." Her voice demanded.

He didn't dare move, though his fingers ached to explore, to find *her* heat, *her* need. But he was twenty, eighteen, sixteen again. Everything he'd learned about controlling his body flew from his mind.

"Hell, Carly." And it wasn't just an expletive, but a truth. The heat, the burn, the want, tortured him. He'd sworn to touch her, please her, make it so good she'd scream for release, and yet his body was so aroused by the newness of woman in his arms that he feared he couldn't go slowly enough.

He bumped foreheads with her, taking deep breaths. He couldn't let go of the ripe curves of her buttocks. "Carly, darlin', I have to tell you it's been a long time since I've been with someone."

She reached up to press a light kiss to his chin. "Hmm."

"I'm, uh, going to have to take this slow." *Find control.*

She twisted her lower body, rubbing her bare skin in his hands against his palms. "Mmm."

Mack gritted his teeth. If they were going to find pleasure in an adult, controlled manner, this had to stop. "You're not helping."

"I don't want to help." Her mouth licked the skin of his neck, and her fingers started unfastening his shirt. She pulled out the tails, dispatched the last button, drew her fingernails in light, horizontal strokes—torturous strokes—across his bare chest to push the shirt off and away.

Mack fought to stay still, and let her small hands

measure him, running from shoulder to waist, then scratching like a little cat up to his flat nipples. She placed her mouth over one, sucking lightly.

Mack groaned, pushed her away urgently. "Honey, honey. You're not helping again."

She smiled a little, running a curious thumb over the hard point she'd made with her mouth. "I told you I don't want to. I've waited a long time for this."

Something told him she meant more than the couple of weeks they'd been arousing each other. "Long time? What exactly do you mean by that?"

She cupped his pectorals, smiling again. "I was twenty, okay? With a very nice young man who was as tired of his virginity as I was."

Every muscle in Mack's body went rigid, including one that was already poker hard. He groaned in plea-sure-pain. "Carly, *no*. Tell me you've had sex since you were twenty."

She didn't look at him. "Nope." Her hands stilled. "Is that a problem?"

Control, control, control. Just barely he kept his fin-gers from biting into the round flesh still in his hands. "Carly, I thought you were a modern woman."

She frowned, and looked at him now. "I *am* a mod-ern woman. Modern women don't take unnecessary risks with their bodies."

He let the shudder overtake him now. It rolled down his arms, and he pulled her closer, bent his head to kiss her. "That's it," he said. "I'm all out of control."

Her mouth burned. It opened for him easily, will-ingly, and he thrust his tongue inside, as if he was worried he'd never get another chance. He shuddered again, the hot, wet taste of her like something he'd never known.

Warmth bloomed on her cheeks, her neck, and he chased it with his fingers, finally going after it from the hemline of her T-shirt. He raced up her ribs and took the heaviness of her breasts into his hands.

He wanted to shout in exultation. The smooth heat of her skin felt new to him, exhilarating in its newness. His thumbs passed over her nipples, and he went dizzy, the knowledge of her arousal making him so damn needy that he wasn't sure he'd last another thirty seconds.

Desperate, he stripped off her shirt and bent to take a nipple in his mouth. He groaned, the sound raw and hungry, as her flavor burst upon his tongue. The fresh, ripe taste made him suck greedily, then rush to her other nipple, his heart pounding, his pulse beating in the unhindered rhythm of youth.

He couldn't remember another woman's touch, texture, fragrance. It was as if it was the first time a woman's breast was against his cheek, her nipple against his tongue. His hands shook so badly he tried twice to grasp the waistband of her shorts, and then, like woman was being revealed to him for the very first time, he watched as his hands slowly drew them away.

His head spun. The blond curls at the juncture of her thighs hid almost nothing. A woman's secrets. Carly was so sweet, so honest, even those were nearly open to him.

Slowly, to enjoy the first touch he could remember, he drew one finger, lightly, gently, over the secret place. She moaned.

He took his gaze from his hand and watched her face instead. This was new and delicious, too. Her lashes fell over her eyes, and her mouth opened on a gasp as he pressed a little deeper, finding folds that opened easily to him.

"My knees are weak," she whispered.

His were, too. But unable to stop touching her, to move any distance, he quickly reached behind him and shut her bedroom door. With one hand cupping her and the other on her shoulder, he turned to press her against the door. When her shoulders bumped against the wood, he bent to take her breast and thrust one finger gently inside her.

His heart jumped at the hot, tight, ready feel of her. Need twisted through him, and when her fingernails scraped down his chest to the waistband of his jeans, he thrust into her again, and then left her breast to take her mouth, his tongue thrusting, too, in a rhythm his body was way too eager to follow.

She was so tight. Her fumbling fingers at his waistband made him think again of her inexperience. The snap popped, and if he didn't stall her he'd not make it any further. To distract her, he breached her secrets with a second finger.

She was so tight.

He kissed her cheek, her ear, her chin, their breaths rushing out. *So tight.* "Honey, how long did you and your twenty-year-old, uh, date?"

He didn't think she heard him at first. Then her eyes opened, focused dazedly on his face. "Once," she said. "Just that one time."

His heart slammed against his chest. His arousal

tried to burst from his jeans. With newfound strength, he swept her into his arms and rushed to the bed.

Pillows, coverlet tumbled to the floor. Need pounded at him. Desire rushed him, pushed him along like it was 10:45 and he had an 11:00 p.m. curfew.

He flung off the rest of his clothes and put on one of the condoms he'd had sense enough to tuck in his wallet, afraid to even look at her. Her naked skin against the white sheets might just do him in.

Hands shaking, he gently opened her thighs and eased himself between them. She pulled him up to her with hot and eager hands. He stopped for pleasure at her breasts, her neck, and then moved to her mouth.

Her taste threw him over the edge. Responding to her demanding hands on his hips, he nudged himself against her, and then thrust in.

She cried out, an ecstatic sound, and arched against him.

Hot, tight, tight, woman, *Carly,* encircled him, took him over, made his body rock into her. Pounding heartbeats sounded in his ears. He drove into her again, and he captured a nipple in his mouth as he surrendered to uncontrollable need.

Good, good, good. *Pleasure,* too tame a word, flamed from their joined bodies over his skin.

Close, so close to the peak, he lifted his head to look at her face. So damn close.

She opened her eyes. "Don't stop now," she said.

But any instant now it would be over, he thought. He was just too close.

"I think you're about to take me to a place I've never been before," she whispered.

He stilled. *Dammit.* She'd never climaxed?

His blood burned even hotter, demanding he flex his hips into her. Once, twice, and it would be all over for him.

His intention to please and pleasure the woman of this frilly, romantic room had been driven away by the young, untried, demanding need she built in him.

"Mack?"

Sweat slicked his shoulders. Gritting his teeth, he pulled away from her a little, though not unlinking them.

"Mack?"

From somewhere he found the strength to control his body. While he wanted to push back into her, find his satisfaction, instead he kissed her soothingly while re-arranging their position. She blushed a little when she found herself spread across his lap, he sitting up against the headboard so that her pretty breasts were just at the level of his mouth.

He was so hard he ached, but the pain was nothing. Not when her moans were so sweet as he sucked again at her breasts and slowly thrust into her while his hand found the hard little pearl between her legs. The man in him smiled at the pleasure he could give her.

The boy she brought out in him still clamored to thrust into her with speed and power.

And then he could tell that's what she needed. She writhed against his body, her voice calling his name, demanding. So he did what they both wanted. With a wet finger he rubbed her most sensitive spot and surrendered to the hard and heavy demands of his blood.

She writhed around him. The clenching of the secret muscles of her body set him off.

When he could breathe again, he inhaled deeply, satisfied by the mingled scents of Carly's perfume and mind-blowing sex. He slid down to the pillows, taking her with him, so that she draped over him, her cheek against his chest, his palm possessive at the small of her back.

Soon he would want her again. Very soon.

He smiled, as that beach-baby song once more floated through his mind. That first-love song.

God. Carly made him new again.

Carly roused from sleep to find Mack kissing her temple. She smiled. He'd woken her just this way shortly after that first, incredible lovemaking, only to arouse her again and then take her swiftly, powerfully, to release.

She turned toward him, only to discover him not between the sheets as she'd expected, but sitting on the edge of the bed, fully dressed.

Her eyes completely opened.

"I have to go home now, honey," he said regretfully. "It's really late."

She captured his hand and brought it to her lips. "I don't care what time it is. Stay." She licked his knuckles. Her desire for him made her want to do the most incredible things.

He groaned. "Carly, you don't know how hard you're making this for me."

She ran a bold hand up his thigh. "How hard?" she said.

He captured her wandering fingers. "Take pity on an old man."

"You don't act like an old man." Carly's body warmed just thinking about what they'd done. What she wanted to do again.

"You don't make me feel like one. But the fact of the matter is, I am." His hand caressed her face. "At the very least I'm a father, and I need to go home so I'll be there when Kimmy wakes up."

An icy fist slammed against her chest. No, not a fist, but her heart, suddenly gone hard and cold.

One of his fingers trailed across her cheek. "But we'll see each other later today. We'll think of something fun to do tonight." He pressed open her mouth to rub the underside of her lower lip. "I'll rack my brain to come up with something even *more* fun for later tonight."

Could a body heat and cool in the same instant?

Carly drew away from Mack's delicious touch and sat up, holding the sheet to her breasts. "Today's Saturday. I have things to do," she said calmly. Going to bed with Mack had been a terrible mistake. She could fall for him if she got too close, stayed too close. "I'll be busy all day."

"Okay." He didn't get it yet. "But how about dinner, say, six? Make it five. I can't wait that long to see you."

"I'm busy tonight, too," Carly said.

"I see." He got it now. He rubbed a hand over his face. "Hell, Carly. What's going on? I know you don't want a relationship, but can't we still see each other?"

"No promises, no pain, remember?" She *had* to protect herself. "See you on Monday, Mack." And leaving him to find his own way out, Carly made an undignified dash for the bathroom before he could see the tears in her eyes.

9

The sluicing hot water washed Mack's scent from her. Carly closed her eyes and tried to pretend she didn't regret losing even that one part of him.

Why hadn't she hung on to her smarts? When he'd come to her door last night, she'd been wary. But the minute he'd touched her, she'd dropped her caution like a butter-fingered birthday girl playing hot potato.

Why?

She edged up the shower's temperature. The answer was as simple as *H* for hot and *C* for cold. She'd dropped her caution for one reason, the big *T*—touch. Because touch—touching him, having Mack touch her—was what she'd wanted since the moment she'd met him.

She sighed heavily and turned toward the shower-head, letting the spray wash over her face. If there were tears, she didn't want to feel them.

Tears, regrets. The minute she took him to her bed, she'd asked for them both. Served her right for choosing the wrong kind of man.

Shampoo in, scrub, rinse out. But Carly had enough brain cells left to know she couldn't wash Mack out of her hair. She turned off the shower, toweled dry and pulled her terry-cloth robe off the hook behind the door.

Her wide-toothed comb slid easily through her wet curls. She wasn't worried about keeping him out of her hair, anyway. She needed to keep him out of her heart.

Achieving that required keeping him out of her bed. So she'd sent him on his way.

She slowly swung open the door, reluctant to face the empty sheets.

And found herself facing Mack instead.

Still fully dressed, he lounged on top of the mussed covers. A white eyelet pillow, shaped like a cloud, was stuffed behind his head. She shut the bathroom door behind her as he crossed his arms over his chest.

"Well?" he asked, one eyebrow raised.

Hedge, Carly. "Well, what?"

"Explain yourself. Explain why you're kicking me out."

She frowned. "I'm not kicking you out. There I was asleep, minding my own business, when you said you had to leave."

"For good." He swung his legs off the bed and put his elbows on his knees. "Then you told me to leave for good."

She sighed. "Mack—"

"Why, Carly?"

"I don't want to get hurt, okay?" she blurted out. "Can you blame me for that?" Surely he would go now.

But he slid her a puzzled look and slowly moved back to his spot against the headboard. She couldn't help it: suddenly Carly pictured herself draped over him like she'd been last night.

"You're not going to distract me that easily, Carly." His voice was hard.

"What?" she croaked. The memory made her hoarse.

"You're not going to look at me with your burning green eyes and make me think of sex instead of truth."

Hot chills licked down her arms. Carly hugged herself, rubbing at them. "I told you the truth," she said. "I don't want to be hurt."

He shook his head slowly. "I don't buy it. Suddenly, after two, count 'em, *two* interludes of unparalleled sex—I see no good reason for modesty here—you decide you want me gone for good."

With a finger he tapped his chin. "What changed between the moment you turned toward my kiss and the moment you turned me toward the door?"

She shrugged and looked out the window. The sky, one shade lighter, hinted at the coming dawn. If she stalled him long enough, he'd have to leave. The way that he could hurt her, the way she'd been hurt in the past, was too intimate, too private to share.

"I remember," he said slowly. "I said I had to go home to Kimmy."

Carly closed her eyes. Last night, when he'd arrived on her doorstep, that's what she'd forgotten. In the midst of her attraction and then her arousal, in the final surrender to all that she'd wanted since the moment she'd met him, she'd forgotten about Kimmy.

"That's it, right? Kimmy."

Silence rose between them. Carly didn't know what

it felt like to him, but to her it was peaceful, comforting. A space and a place to hide within and behind.

"I'm going to make you talk about it."

Carly pursed her lips. Obviously silence wouldn't cut it with him.

But how *could* he make her talk about it? She set her mouth to a stubborn line and looked him straight in the eye. "I'm not going to," she said.

He stared at her right back. "You don't like my little girl."

Carly's heart jerked. "No!" God, she couldn't let him believe that! "Kimmy's wonderful. Sweet. She's—" *Smug* wrote itself over his face.

"Gotcha." His expression turned even smugger.

Heat crawled through Carly's insides. Not sexual heat, but anger, real anger. "Don't you think you got me."

She was so mad she could spit, or maybe, like Grits the cat, so mad she could eat a snake. "How I feel isn't something to smile about or trick me about, you understand?"

He sat up straighter. "No, Carly, I don't understand. But I want to."

He didn't cool her mood and the words rushed out. "Yeah? You think you want to understand? Do you think you want to know that when I said goodbye to Peter I said goodbye to his daughter, too?" Carly's fists clenched at the familiar pain.

"Peter has a daughter?"

Carly stared out the window and wished the dawn could lighten her heart like it lightened the sky. "I didn't tell you that part, did I? Peter's daughter is Laurel.''

Mack interrupted the silence by clearing his throat. ''You spent a lot of time with her?''

Even as Carly watched, the sky brightened. ''I loved her. From the very beginning I connected with Laurel. We loved books and dolls and...''

''She reminded you of you?''

She barely heard him. ''Maybe. Her mother—Peter's ex—had agreed to be the leader of Laurel's Brownie troop. But when a work commitment got in the way I took—''

''Over.'' He'd moved to the edge of the bed now, closer to Carly.

She inched nearer the window. ''I was happy to. So we spent more time together. Evenings, even when Peter couldn't join us for dinner. Holidays when he had custody. I tried to make them special memories for her.'' A deep breath didn't reach all the way to her lungs. ''And—and when Peter asked me to marry him...''

She purposely waited, wanting Mack to fill in the blanks. But he said nothing, damn him. Then he reached out to stroke over the top of her hand with a long finger.

Carly stopped trying to look away from him. She stopped trying to not tell the truth. ''And when Peter asked me to marry him I began to think of Laurel as my daughter, too.''

With the words out, familiar pain took its best punch at her stomach. Carly felt the sting of tears, blinked them away.

"Honey." Mack raked his hands through his hair, a frustrated, almost angry gesture. "So when Peter left your life he took Laurel with him."

"That's what hurt," Carly whispered hoarsely. "That's what broke my heart."

Mack heard the first song of a bird and wanted to throttle something—Peter, or the dove that signaled it was really morning, or his own conscience that pressed him to be home before Kimmy awoke. He took hold of one of Carly's pillows instead. Squeezed the thing dead.

"God, I'm sorry, Carly."

She looked at him as if she was surprised he was still there. One shoulder lifted. "I have plenty of pillows."

Frustrated anger pricked him again. Did she think he couldn't understand her feelings? "I'm sorry about *Laurel,* Carly."

"Yeah," she said.

He could tell she didn't think he got it. "I'm *really* sorry, okay? You seem to think I don't see how you were hurt."

"Thank you." Her voice was quiet.

And so dismissive it brought him to his feet. "Dammit, Carly." He grabbed her arm. "I'm not as dense as you think. When you told me about Peter last night I saw right away that losing *him* hadn't hurt you. I knew it was something else."

Her eyes were more gray than green right now. More unshed tears than untouched passion. And she was quiet, too quiet. He shook her arm a little. "You believe me, right? Admit I understand."

"If you do, great." She swallowed. "Because then you understand why I won't be with you anymore. Why I refuse to take that risk again."

Mack poured himself a cup of coffee and cleared his throat. "The worst part of it is, what could I say to that?"

No one in the kitchen answered.

"Was I going to make some promise to her?" He slapped the carafe back on the burner. Coffee sloshed over the edge and ran down the glass to sizzle against the heat. "I'm in the exact same position as that Peter was. *Not* that there's a chance I'll get back with Suzanne—not a chance in hell—but I'm a man with a child and a lousy track record when it comes to women."

He swigged a gulp from his mug and welcomed the blackness and the caffeine. "So I bowed to her wishes. Said I wouldn't bother her again."

He turned away from his early-morning companions to stare out across the pool. "And she was grateful. Cool and grateful." Another gulp of coffee didn't dispell the bad taste in his mouth.

He spun back. "Hell. Can you believe it? After a night of the best sex in my life, the woman is grateful when I *leave*."

Grits the cat eyed him with disdainful interest. His tail swished impatiently.

Thank God for Corndog. By contrast, the yellow Lab whined in sympathy. There was a reason they called dogs man's best friend.

Another tail swish from Grits.

"Oh, come on, cat," Mack answered. "What was left to do? I couldn't say I loved the woman."

He took another scalding gulp of coffee. "You and I both know that's a heap of romantic dog sh—sorry, Corndog—romantic *hogwash* made up by greeting card companies and Brad Pitt's fan club."

Grits blinked one eye and then the other.

Mack looked away. *I couldn't say I loved the woman.*

Carly ran her thumb beneath the flap of the vermillion envelope that came in the day's mail. She'd dried her eyes by sunup and made a lot of headway packing in the morning hours.

She sank to a box filled with kitchen linens and pulled a greeting card from the envelope she knew came from her mother. No Sherlocking there, the return address had been the number of the house she grew up in.

Inside the card was another card, sealed, with Laurel's name scrawled across the envelope. On several occasions her mother had met Laurel and fallen for the little girl, too. The envelope most likely contained a birthday card.

Laurel turned nine next week.

Carly tilted the open card, the one addressed to her, this way and that, trying to get a good read of her mother's loopy handwriting. "Neato Laurel's address. Plastered send on my birthday washes." Wrong.

Carly squinted. "Need Laurel's address. Please send on my birthday wishes," she finally read.

In the corner of the couch, still in the bag, sat the

birthday gift she'd bought at the mall for Laurel the day before. Even as she'd purchased it, she hadn't been sure she would mail it. But it had enchanted Carly—a beautifully bound set of Laura Ingalls Wilder's *Little House* books. If she knew Laurel—and she really, really did—the girl would treasure them forever.

After reading them cover to cover to cover to cover.... There were nearly a dozen books.

With a flick of her wrist, she sailed the birthday card in the direction of the gift. It would only take her minutes to wrap the present, and then she could take both the card and the package to the post office for mailing.

But should she intrude on Laurel's life? What was to be gained by showing she still cared?

Carly idly glanced at her mother's card to her. On the front, one of those hokey country landscapes with an old farm house and a beat-up mailbox. Probably purchased at the Dime-and-Drug, Spenser, Indiana's answer to Wal-Mart.

Inside, along with her mother's nearly illegible writing, was the card's sentiment, expressed in tiny, light gray type. "To find love, you must first give love away."

As sentiments went, it was pretty hokey, too. But she decided to take the "give" as an omen. Laurel really *would* enjoy the books. After a quick trip to the post office, Carly promised herself she'd get back to packing.

Considering the situation with Mack, it was imperative she get out of the big city and away from men like him—men with big-time baggage—as soon as possible.

Monday morning Carly drove to Mack's house and noted the cars parked out front and in the driveway. *Ouch.* She'd forgotten about the meeting scheduled with the Cycle programmers, Gary and Bruce. Lisa would be there, too, as they went over the final details of the wooing trip. Carly and Mack's flight to San Francisco took off Wednesday at the crack of dawn. Muscle Machines, Inc. expected them at 10 a.m.

She parked her car on the street and hurried up the front walk, disgruntled at being the last one there. How would it go, facing Mack in a roomful of Cycle employees?

It would go fine! *It must go fine.* Okay, so there might be a quick burst of embarrassment, but after that she'd be able to settle down to business. The whole point of breaking off with Mack had been to keep any discomfort to a minimum.

She rapped calmly on the front door. From a distance Mack called, "Come in!" Determined to appear unruffled, she pushed open the door and turned left to walk quickly toward the office, at the same time doing a final tuck and smooth of her shirt, then a readjustment of the side seams of her skirt with a little wriggle of her hips.

"Where you going?" From nearby, Mack's voice again.

Carly froze. She didn't even get the benefit of another deep inhale before she spied him, and then everyone else—Lisa, Bruce and Gary—gazing at her from the living room.

"I thought we'd meet in here instead of the office," Mack explained. "There are more seats."

Carly executed an about-face and walked slowly toward the living room, ignoring the wave of heat on her face. Maybe nobody had noticed her private sartorial ritual.

"Whazzat bump-and-grind thing called?" Bruce grinned and made a play of handing over his coffee mug to Mack. "Don't think I'll be needing this anymore, boss. I'm all woke up."

Maybe nobody would notice if she killed Bruce dead.

"Watch out, Bruce, I haven't had *my* caffeine yet this morning." She grinned back at the programmer, a baring of her teeth. "It makes me mean."

She found her coffee mug pressed into her hand. Mack had filled it from a thermal carafe on the table. "Was that my mistake?" he said softly, for only her ears. "I should have fed you coffee first?"

Carly sipped at the brew—prepared her way, with a splash of nonfat milk—and pretended she didn't hear him. She didn't even look at him. Instead of taking the obvious and open seat, beside Mack on the couch, she opted for perching on the arm of Lisa's overstuffed chair. "How's the work-at-home life?" she asked her friend.

Lisa looked at Carly, looked at Mack, did the whole her-to-him glance again. The three men began discussing a recent coding problem. Lisa hunched her shoulder

away from the group and narrowed her eyes at Carly.
"What's going on?" she half whispered.

It couldn't be that transparent. Not when she was
working so hard at appearing unbothered. "Nothing,"
Carly tried. "Besides Bruce being his usual obnoxious
self."

"There's a vibration in this room that wasn't here a
few minutes ago."

Carly shrugged. "Oh, yeah? You might want to
mention it to Mack. There's a snake missing around
here, and maybe you're sensing its presence."

Lisa's eyes widened, and her feet lifted off the floor.
"I don't like snakes."

And then, thank goodness, Mack asked a question
that drew Lisa and her into the conversation.

Half an hour later Carly slipped into the kitchen for
a glass of water. The ice rattling into the glass apparently hid the sound of Mack's footsteps, because suddenly he was in the kitchen, too.

He smelled good—citrusy and clean—and she remembered the fragrance upon her sheets, the faint hint
of it in her hair that morning before she'd shampooed
it away.

"Are you okay?" he asked quietly.

"Of course I'm okay." *Of course* she was.

"Fine." He shrugged and calmly took his own glass
out of the cabinet.

Suddenly *his* coolness bugged her. It bugged her that
he might not think she was okay. His good smell
bugged her. The fact that he wanted a glass of water
bugged her.

"What about you?" she said. "Are *you* okay?"

He turned toward her, surprise on his face. "Me? Why wouldn't I be okay?"

Another flare of annoyance kindled in her belly, and she set down her glass, then crossed her arms over her chest. "Why wouldn't *I* be okay? Same reason."

He lifted one hand in surrender. "So we're both okay. Good." His glass tilted and he took a long drink.

Carly watched the muscles of his throat work. She followed the smooth movement down to the open neck of his short-sleeved shirt. He turned his head a bit and she gasped.

"What?"

Carly's face went hot. "Maybe...maybe you should button up your shirt."

His fingers touched the second button, firmly fastened. "It's fine."

She clenched her own hands together. "The other one. Higher up."

"Like this?" Frowning, he brought the two edges of his collar together. "Is this some fashion statement I'm unaware of? It's not very comfortable."

Heat waved over her face again. "There's, um, a little mark...maybe you nicked yourself shaving."

He frowned again. "I didn't shave this morning, Carly."

Well, duh. She should have seen that. A sexy burr shadowed his jaw.

"I haven't slept well the past couple of nights. The Kimmy-alarm jumped on my bed this morning about fifteen minutes after I fell asleep and about thirty minutes before this morning's meeting."

She thought about dropping the whole subject. But

if he turned his head a certain way, the others would see the mark on his neck, and Lisa, romance happy, might just put that mark and those "vibrations" together and then they'd never hear the end of it. Gone would be her whole plan of appearing unruffled and unaffected.

She gestured with a finger in the direction of his neck. "You have a bruise." With difficulty she swallowed, then lowered her voice. "A passion bruise."

Understanding dawned in his eyes. "Ah." Then he laughed softly. "A *passion bruise,* huh?"

The conversation was starting to take a wrong turn. She could feel it. Grabbing up her glass, she made to return to the living room.

Mack caught her arm. "I like that." He laughed again. *"Passion bruise."*

"I should get back in there," she said, tugging on her arm. "They'll start to wonder."

He didn't let go. "And well they might. Mack with a hickey—excuse me, *passion bruise.* Carly walking through the front door with a wriggle."

She closed her eyes. "Mack, please."

His hand was hot on her, and then his thumb began to move, to softly caress the underside of her arm. "What are you thinking about when we're in there?"

The conversation's wrong turn was becoming dangerous. "I'm thinking about work," she said. "About ironing out the details of our trip."

"Oh, yeah. The *wooing* trip." He smiled. "I happen to think we're ready. All the details are flat as pancakes. So I'm in there thinking about you, Carly. About your mouth *bruising* me. About the places I think I left some marks.''

Chills ran cold over Carly's hot skin. She'd never seen Mack like this, so intense. So intent on making her uncomfortable.

''Don't make this harder for me, Mack.'' She tugged at her arm again, and this time he let go.

He grimaced. ''That's all I want you to admit, okay? Admit that it's a little hard. That you're not as calm, cool and collected as you look.''

She wanted to giggle hysterically. Maybe she *was* leaving Southern California too early. Just when her acting skills were ripening.

''It's not easy,'' she admitted. ''But it's best.''

He looked at her closely, then nodded, slamming his water glass so hard against the countertop she was surprised it didn't shatter.

Then he started out of the kitchen.

''Wait. Aren't you going to do anything about your...neck?''

He reached up and, pushing aside his collar, unerringly found the mark. His finger traced over it lightly. ''I like it,'' he said.

Those chills pricked over her skin again. Un-cool, un-calm, un-collected chills. Hot chills. *Damn him.*

He started past her. Suddenly she couldn't let it go. She wanted to wield her own power, to make him as bothered as he made her. Reaching out, she put her hand on his arm. ''About the meeting...''

Eyebrows raised, he halted. From his neutral expression, she could tell he thought her remark would be business related. ''I just thought you'd like to know.

When *I* got dressed this morning I had to change twice. To keep what you'd left on me...*private.*''

His eyes were changing already, going from brown to burning black.

''Because you're right, Mack, you marked me, too. One passion bruise.'' She touched her chest, at the rise of her breast just left of her heart. ''Here.''

Then she preceded him out the door, giving her hips just the tiniest of torturing wriggles.

10

After the meeting broke up, Carly headed for the office down the hall. Despite the pancake-flat details, there was still work to do before Wednesday's departure: another look at the specs for the treadmill program they'd present to Muscle Machines and a series of phone calls to the other product teams to ensure their readiness for a few days without her or Mack.

Phone to her ear, she was checking with the stationary bicycle group when Mack walked in and sat down at the computer terminal. Avoiding his gaze, she kept the conversation with the beta-tester, Fernando, going longer than necessary. She wasn't ready for Mack, four walls and nothing else.

Call over, the click of receiver to phone sounded as loud as a bomb blast to her ears. She froze. Mack stilled. An unspoken *What now?* screeched into the rushing silence.

Carly considered an early, long lunch, but they'd scheduled a conference call to Germany with John in forty-five minutes.

Her breath sounded loud in the room, and she tried controlling it, inhaling lightly, exhaling through pursed lips.

"What the hell are you doing?" he asked harshly, not turning around. "That noise is grating on my nerves."

"Excuse me," Carly said, the anger she'd felt toward him in the kitchen resurfacing. "I'm breathing."

He shifted his shoulders and stabbed at the computer keys, screen after screen of data scrolling by.

Ignoring him, Carly stomped over to the room's closet and pulled open the door. To one side of a stack of semifilled boxes sat a metal file cabinet. Carly grabbed the handle of the top drawer to slide it open. *Scr-ee-e-ech.* Mack flinched. Carly ignored that, too, and retrieved the marketing folders prepared for Wednesday's meeting.

With her elbow, she slammed shut the metal drawer with a *rrroosh-clang,* then nudged the closet door half-shut. The folders hit the worktable with a slap.

Mack didn't bother stifling a long-suffering sigh.

She huffed one back in return, then tried to work.

Pretended to work.

From the corner of her eye, Carly saw screens of data zip over Mack's computer monitor. He couldn't be gleaning a thing from the flying data. The words in front of her were just as unintelligible.

Each of her breaths shotgunned into the tense silence. Finally she couldn't take it anymore. "This is exactly why what happened shouldn't have," she said. "You're making me crazy."

"You made me crazy before we did what you think we shouldn't have." His voice was angry, too. "But you're right, it's worse now."

"I should have said no."

"For God's sake, don't blame yourself," Mack said, sounding like that was exactly what he was doing. "I shouldn't have pushed you."

"Pushed me?" Carly's hands fisted. "Don't think I can be pushed into anything."

He swung around to confront her. "Face it, I have more experience—"

"So you think you seduced me? Give me a break." Carly blew her bangs out of her eyes with impatience. "I know my own mind, Mack."

He flung up his hand in a dismissive gesture. "Forget it."

"I'm trying," she retorted.

The anger bubbled, along with a sense of futility. Working together, traveling together, spelled disaster with a big *D*. She glared at him in frustration. He glared back.

And then over Mack's shoulder, in the direction of the closet, something caught her eye. A small, low, *slithery* movement.

Slithery.

Snakes slithered.

Carly narrowed her eyes. *Oh.* Poking out of the half-open closet door was the head of a snake.

Oh, yuck. Poking out of the head of the snake was the hindquarters—tail wiggling—of a mouse. Carly slid back in her chair and pulled her feet to the seat. "Eek," she said faintly, pointing. "Mouse."

Mack spun around his chair, then froze. "That's no mouse, that's a snake."

"The President?"

Mack still didn't move. "Yeah."

"But he has a mouse," Carly said. "Do something. I don't like mice."

Mack continued to sit in his chair, hands on his knees, like a breathing rendition of the *Lincoln Memorial* statue.

"Are you just going to sit there?" Carly watched the back half of the mouse struggle with horrified fascination. "What if he lets that rodent go?"

"Um…"

"Go grab that snake!"

"I, uh… Hell, Carly. I gotta tell you I don't like snakes."

"What?"

"Hate 'em."

"What?"

"I ha—"

"I heard you," she said, staring. "I just don't believe you. What kind of man has a snake and is afraid of them?"

"Hey, Indiana Jones didn't like snakes," Mack defended. "Nobody thinks any less of *him.*"

Carly huffed. "Well, he didn't *own* any, either."

"This is Dad's snake. The President and I have only a nodding acquaintance."

Another little silence fell over the room as they observed snake and mouse. Carly hoped Mack was contemplating some sort of rescue-slash-capture. The only thing she could think about was the bloodcurdling possibilities of a reptile and a rodent loose in a twenty-by-fourteen room.

With a slow, slow movement, Mack reached over and tipped the plastic waste can onto the floor. With his foot, he nudged it gently toward the closet. "Are you pondering what I'm pondering?" he asked aloud.

Carly remembered their first meeting. His gorgeous smile, his slam-bang impact on her senses, the "Pinky and the Brain" cartoon tie he'd been wearing. Whenever lab mouse Brain came up with another plan to take over the world, he always asked his partner Pinky that same question: "Are you pondering what I'm pondering?" She'd said those same words to Mack that day.

Carly couldn't help the smile that broke over her face. "I think so, Brain. But how are we going to teach moon rocks to fly?" Poor, befuddled Pinky never was on Brain's same wavelength.

Mack shot her an appreciative, laughing glance that he rapidly changed to Brain's maniacal leer. "Pinky, I'm going to have to hurt you soon."

Chills shot down Carly's spine. Not ugh-there's-a-mouse goose bumps, but premonitory—maybe *post*-monitory ones. *Carly* could be hurt soon. Maybe was already.

"Why don't you get up slowly and shut the office door, okay, Carly? Just in case my plan doesn't work, at least The President won't get out of the room."

"I'm more worried about the mouse," Carly grumbled, but with quiet movements, she did as asked.

Mack had slowly risen from his chair. He rolled up a thick computer printout, then with one quick movement, shooed the snake into the trash can and set it back on its end. The printout was slapped on top of the can. Carly rushed over and clapped a dictionary on top of the paper report to keep The President from pushing it aside.

Heart beating like a rock drummer, Carly looked at Mack. She grinned. "My hero!"

Grinning back, he high-fived her upstretched hand.

At that instant of flesh striking flesh, something inside Carly died.

If only it was the attraction that had died.

But it wasn't, she acknowledged ruefully. What had turned up its toes was the anger. She couldn't maintain that safe anger anymore. Not toward a grinning, heroic, snake-fearing, great-smelling, big bad dad.

Mack scraped a hand over his face and stared across the small table in his hotel room at Carly. "Why don't you go to bed?"

She looked as exhausted as he felt. After all day at Muscle Machines, Inc. they'd come back to the hotel to crunch numbers. MM, Inc. wanted some changes to the basic treadmill software package and they expected the additional costs to be outlined at tomorrow's 9:00 a.m. meeting.

"I'm okay. Fine," Carly replied, her standard response to almost every question he'd asked her since the snake-and-mouse debacle two days before.

Okay. Fine. They'd met, been combustibly attracted, worked together, slept together, and now they did nothing together but mumble okay-fines and together pretend that the past three weeks had never happened.

He'd been angry about it at first. Angry that he'd given in to the need to sink into her hot, soft body. Angry at how disappointed he'd been when she'd said

"Not again." You'd think his past would have prepared him for another woman who wouldn't follow through.

But follow through how? The anger had evaporated when he'd admitted to himself that he didn't know *what* he wanted from her.

With a sigh she tried tucking a soft curl back into the twist confining her hair. The frothy lock immediately sprang free to brush her cheek.

Mack curbed the urge to stroke its softness, too. "Go to bed, honey."

The endearment slipped out, and her head immediately lifted. "Not until we're finished. John wants Muscle Machines and I'm going to make sure Cycle gets their business."

His eyebrows rose at her fierceness. "Such loyalty."

She shrugged and started clicking the keys of her laptop computer. "It's my last assignment for John. I owe it to him for all the opportunities he's given me."

Her last assignment. Remembering that had kept any wayward impulses of his under control. He had to congratulate himself for that.

The phone rang. It was at Carly's elbow, so at his nod, she picked it up. "Hi, Kimmy."

Mack checked his watch. After 9:00 p.m. Kimmy should be in bed.

He held out his hand for the receiver.

Carly shook her head. "You wanted to talk to me?" she asked. "What's the matter, couldn't you sleep?"

With several deep nods, Carly listened intently. Mack took pleasure in her face, the freckles dusting her cheeks. He'd never had the chance to count them, and he closed his eyes against the disappointed pang.

"The blue one. With the red ribbon." Carly listened again and shook her head as if Kimmy could see her. "Granddad does a fine job with a ponytail. But Daddy will be home with his French braiding fingers soon, sweetie. You want to tell him good-night? Here."

Carly's hand brushed Mack's—sizzling warmth—as she passed him the phone.

He listened to his daughter's excited chatter. A special field trip the next day. The need for Carly's advice for the best, most *george*-ous outfit.

The need for Carly. He smiled and spoke soothingly to Kimmy, hoping to make her bedtime calm for his father's sake. But she babbled on excitedly, even when he gave the dozenth command that it was time for bed. Looking at the work yet to do and feeling guilty that his father had to face the nighttime chatterbox, Mack's shoulders tensed. Numbers required crunching, his daughter required soothing, and his tired brain didn't feel up to both jobs.

"Let me," Carly said, surprising Mack by taking the phone from his hand.

Wearing a bemused, tender smile on her face she quickly talked Kimmy into heading for her room, her pillow and her stuffed menagerie.

He relaxed as he watched Carly, fascinated by her face and her ability to cajole his daughter to sleep. Sharing the task felt strange—but good. He sighed away the last of his stress. He couldn't remember the last time he'd let someone take on one of his responsibilities. And the woman who had unburdened him would be gone from his life in a few days.

That thought held no congratulations at all.

"We did it!" Carly's fierce whisper and her smile clung to Mack's soul as strongly as her fingers to his arm. They walked into the lobby-level restaurant of their San Francisco hotel, ready to celebrate the successful completion of their negotiations with the MM, Inc. team.

He wished she wasn't wearing the black-and-white dress. It was scoop-necked, sophisticated and little. She looked like a self-assured, successful businesswoman. Yet she still smelled like Carly, fresh, sweet and…something else. Suddenly he remembered her bedroom, white lace, fluffy pillows and flounces.

Carly smelled like romance.

The contrast of sophistication and sweetness hit his head like one too many rum-and-umbrella drinks. Dizzy for a minute, he halted, and she looked up at him, another smile rivaling her blond froth of hair for dazzle. From somewhere came the distant notes of the beach-baby song.

"Oh!" Carly said, still beaming. "There's dancing!"

Mack breathed a sigh of relief. So that was the source of the music. A band. For a moment he'd thought it came from his heart.

Andrea Giovanni, the petite and unlikely president of Muscle Machines, stood up to welcome them toward her table. Drink orders were taken, appetizers passed around, and Mack silently sipped his Jack Daniels on the rocks while the women on either side of him, Carly and Andrea, chatted like old friends.

Carly told Andrea of her plans to return to Indiana. "I can't believe John's letting you go!" the other woman exclaimed.

I can't believe he is, either, Mack grumbled to himself. Somebody should exert more pressure to keep her at Cycle.

Over entrées of chicken for him, artichoke pasta for Carly and prime rib for Andrea, the two women lamented their single states and men in general. Mack tried not to listen by engaging one of the VPs in a discussion of children—they both had preschool girls. Above their exchanged laughter over tickle-me toys and beanbag beasties, though, Mack could still hear Andrea and Carly.

"Intimidated by a successful woman," said dark-haired Andrea. "And afraid of my five brothers."

"Willing to take you into their life," replied Carly with a frown. "But only so far."

Only so far? What the hell did that mean? Wasn't it she who had cut off any further exploration between the two of them?

By dessert, *crème brûlée* for him, something chocolate for the other six at the table, Mack found himself steaming. The women had amused themselves with tales of romances-gone-sour for the entire meal. Mack knew that any minute he'd star in one of Carly's stories.

"And *then*—" Her gaze darted his way and she hastily closed her mouth.

Mack had segued from kids' toys to kids' soccer to

private schools versus public schools. He was tired of keeping up his end of the conversation—all revolving around fatherhood. He was tired of being seen as the nice dad but bad romance.

Damn, was he tired of being only the dad, the boss, the son, the pet keeper, the homeowner. All those roles that burden him hour-by-hour, day-by-day.

Carly's hand was waving as she made some love-gone-awry point to Andrea. He grabbed it. "Let's dance," he said abruptly.

Carly stared at him as he pulled her from her seat. Something mischievous brightened Andrea's eyes, and she caught Carly's white linen napkin before it fell to the floor. "They're playing your song, Carly," she said.

On the small dance floor, Mack held Carly in his arms.

She didn't melt all over him like he wished she would. A businesslike eight inches separated them. "Do you think this is wise?" she whispered. "We should probably stay at the table. Or you should have asked Andrea to dance first."

"I didn't want to dance with Andrea."

Her eyes widened as he dragged her four inches closer. "This is a *business* dinner," she said.

"The business was concluded at four this afternoon when they signed the contract. This is a celebration. And how I want to celebrate is dancing with you."

"But—" She broke off as she noticed the MM, Inc. team leaving the table. They waved goodbye. Mack thought he saw Andrea wink.

Carly lifted her hand to wave a return farewell. "But—"

"Shh." He hauled her closer and pressed her head against his shoulder. "They've left. Just relax."

He felt a shuddering sigh ripple through Carly.

The waxed wood floor slid easily beneath his feet. The band played something big yet understated— Mack's father would certainly know the tune—but it had enough of a beat that Carly's hips picked it up and began to sway beneath his hands.

Damn. Heat spiraled up his arms and arrowed straight to his groin. He went hard.

So did his resolve.

He was tired of being the negotiator. Tired of being only a father. Tired of being cautious, sensible, responsible.

Tired of racing toward middle age.

He wanted to take Carly's hand and step off the track. Just for tonight meander away from the path.

He wanted her again, not in any of his many roles, but just for himself.

He wanted to celebrate by taking Carly to bed and making slow, sweet, sinuous love.

The dance ended with a final shivery flourish of the cymbals. Carly stopped, but Mack's hands tightened at her waist.

She closed her eyes and rested her forehead against his shoulder. Could he feel the pounding beat of her heart? Did he realize that if he let go, her jelly knees might just not hold her up?

"We'll be taking a short break," the bandleader said into the mike.

Carly reluctantly pulled out of Mack's embrace. Would he see sadness written all over her now? Because the suffocating weight of endings and goodbyes had sat on her chest all evening.

No more Cycle.

No more Mack.

When their flight took off the next morning, all that would be left for her to do in L.A. was to clear some things out of Mack's office and finish the final packing at her apartment.

Then a goodbye to a few friends, her co-workers, Kimmy, Ray, the animals, Mack.

Mack.

He didn't let go of her hand as they headed back to their table. His fingers threaded hers, and she let the delicious response to his touch tickle over her skin. Tonight she wouldn't deny it. She'd merely enjoy these last few minutes with him before they parted at their respective hotel room doors.

He pressed her evening purse into her free hand and led her to the lobby of the hotel.

In the elevator he stared ahead with his head tilted back, watching the ascending floor numbers light. "I want you."

"Excuse me?" Carly, in a strange daze of part warmth and part regret, thought she didn't catch all he said. "You want me to what?"

"I want to have you naked and moaning in my bed and keep you that way all night long."

Prickly chills burst over her skin. *"Mack."* Then

Carly remembered where she was and looked wildly about her.

The elevator was empty except for the two of them. "I, um…"

He didn't look at her. "Don't answer now. You have fourteen more floors to think about it."

Anticipation and exhilaration rose in her at the same rate as the elevator. Could she do it? *Should* she do it?

She wanted to. She'd been aching to since the instant he'd left her bed the last time.

But moaning and naked in his bed might mean exposing her heart, too.

Her pulse pounding hotly, she stared at his handsome, clean profile. In a few days she'd be gone, away from Mack, away from the risk.

His hand was hard and hot in hers. She thought of it on her body, of his mouth against hers, and her wild rush of hormones was going faster now, faster than the speeding elevator.

With two floors yet to go she squeezed his hand and hoarsely whispered. "Yes," she said. "I say yes."

He looked at her now, and the fierce, dark blaze of his eyes might have scared her, but it didn't. She offered her mouth to him willingly. She knew this man. She trusted him with herself.

And she found out that he knew her, too.

Once inside his room, the door clicked loudly, finally, behind them. Carly's heart jerked, but as if he knew it might, Mack was right there, kissing her temple softly. "Don't be afraid," he whispered in the darkness. "Let me take care of you."

But if she thought that "naked and moaning" in his

bed meant a replay of the hot carnality of their first time together, Carly was wrong. Mack was in a different mood this night, unhurried, gentle.

"You smell good," he said, and he drew the pins from her hair to sift it through his hands. He held the curly mass off her nape and kissed her sweetly there, then rubbed his cheek against the kissed spot, as if he could press the caress into her flesh.

At the foot of the bed, he knelt to take off her shoes, then ran a lingering hand up her legs to the top of her panty hose. He drew them off, catching her silky underpants in his thumbs to pull them away, too.

But he didn't touch her any more intimately. Instead he stood and took her in his arms, kissing her like a movie star kisses the starlet, openmouthed and eager, but unhurried, as if the director wanted the kiss from a thousand different camera angles. His hands moved over her body so that the satiny lining of her dress slid over her sensitized, naked skin.

Beneath her dress and her bra, Carly's breasts felt hot and overdressed. She rubbed them against his chest while pushing his suit jacket to the floor and fumbling with his tie.

He didn't let up on the kiss. She took his warm and wicked tongue into her mouth, time and again, trying to hold on to enough sense to get the frustrating tie out of the way.

They both gasped for air when he lifted his mouth. Finally done with the tie, Carly stared in the darkness at the formidable row of buttons on his dress shirt. "You're going to have to do them," she said. "My hands—they're shaking too much."

His, lean and warm, gathered up her fingers. The silly, trembling things were taken into his mouth one by one, sucked and tongued until she slid down to the mattress, needy. "Mack, *please.*"

But he didn't respond to her plea. Instead he carried on with the thorough, gentle invasion of his touch. Somehow he got her bra off while leaving her dress on. He touched her over the dress, under the dress, kissed her wrists, her elbows, told her how much he appreciated her scent, her texture, her ankles, her knees.

His tongue drew a slow, tantalizing path up the back of her legs, and then he started whispering again as he took off the rest of his clothes and finally, finally released the zipper of her dress.

She was a warm ooze of desire now, a liquid woman who readily flowed over his body as he touched her slowly, gently, while speaking urgently against her ear of hard heat and aching want, of being made young by the sound of her moans and the sound of a love song that only he seemed to hear.

What they had in that bed and in that dark was everything she'd always wanted. The fussiness, the frills, the quiet whispers and the low groans. The romance of sex. The sex of romance.

And how he'd discovered her need for it she didn't know.

She flew apart in his arms and then let him gather her back up. For a few minutes they dozed, then he woke her with a slow kiss and carried her into the shower. The bathroom was hot and steamy after he washed her.

Just before leading her back to the bed, he looked at

the fogged mirror over the sink and flashed her a sweet, wicked grin.

With one finger he wrote Mack + Carly. Then he drew a fat, lopsided heart around their names.

That was how and when she lost hers.

She decided to exact her revenge as their warm bodies hit the cool sheets.

He started talking. "Let me—" again, but she pressed her fingers over his mouth.

"My turn," she said, and pinned him to the bed with her body.

Mack took too much on himself, including the responsibility for both their pleasure. Her tongue ran over his chest, ran down through the light chest hair that led to the hot, smooth-yet-hard strength of him.

He tasted powerful against her tongue. Mack tried protesting—he wanted to take over again—but she firmly held him down and loved him with her mouth and her heart.

Shudders ran through him when it was over. "Carly," he whispered hoarsely, *"Carly."*

She grinned to herself. She'd made him speechless.

But only for a moment. "You shouldn't...you didn't..."

She grinned again. He still wasn't coherent. "I took care of you," she said. "I wanted to give to you."

He stared at her blankly.

Her heart began a pulsing ache. "Oh, Mack," she said. "Doesn't anybody ever make it easier for you?"

He shook his head slowly—in denial? In bewilderment?—then he drew her up against him for a tender kiss.

11

I'm going to tell Mack I'm in love with him.

In the seat beside him on the plane, Carly held his hand tightly. She didn't think he'd be displeased.

She even hoped he would be happy.

The flight attendant crackled over the speaker that they should prepare for arrival at L.A. International Airport.

After last night, he certainly wouldn't be surprised.

"Mack, I—"

He turned his head and opened his eyes. Tired darkness. His mouth—so tempting, so knowing—curved up at the corners. "What, honey?"

"I..."

He rubbed the knuckles of their entwined hands against her cheek. "Spit it out."

A male flight attendant rushed up the aisle, rattling a tray holding empty glasses. The wheels of the plane touched down with a bump. Mack's head was so close to hers that they bonked. In the ensuing "ouch-rub" the moment and her bravery was lost.

She'd do it on the taxi ride home.

But the driver was garrulous and a San Francisco native. Mack's warmth brushed her shoulder, and she looked up at him. While answering the driver's home-town query, Mack winked and smiled.

At his house. She'd tell him there. The taxi would drop them off and before she even unlocked the door of her car, which she'd left in front, she would look up and say, "I love you." She practiced it in her mind. Imagined his expression, the way he'd kiss her after she said the words.

A shiver tracked down her spine.

"You cold?" he whispered.

She shook her head but nonetheless burrowed closer when he put his arm around her. After she told him she loved him, after the imagined kiss, she would convince Ray and Kimmy that they all deserved ice-cream sundaes, her treat.

Kimmy liked extra whipped cream and two cherries. The little girl had let this vital information slip during one of their afternoon talks. Carly smiled. She might go for extras herself. Another happy shiver ran through her, and she settled back against Mack's relaxed body. Oh, this was going to be good.

Two houses away from Mack's, tension suddenly stiffened his muscles. He straightened out of his sprawl. "Damn," he said under his breath. "Damn, damn, *damn*."

"What?"

But the cab had stopped behind her car, and he was already out the door. Carly shoved some bills into the driver's hand and followed Mack up the walk, noting the unfamiliar sedan parked in the driveway.

The front door banged open. "Kimmy! Dad!" Mack yelled. Then he halted in the entry.

Carly skidded to a stop, just millimeters short of slamming into his back. To see what he was looking at, she had to step aside and peer around his shoulder.

Kimmy was on the living room floor, playing with a doll in Caribbean-style dress. Mack's father sat in the easy chair nearby, Grits on his lap. A slim, dark-haired woman perched on the couch, an uneasy expression on her face.

"Suzanne," Mack said tersely. "Long time no see."

"I know." The pretty woman fluttered her hands. "Ray said you were out of town. I came by to see Kimmy."

At the sound of her name, the little girl looked up with a sunny smile. "See, Daddy?" she said, holding up the doll. "See what Mommy brought me?"

As if someone had yanked the lacy curtains from her bedroom windows, Carly blinked against a blinding glare. Even voices hurt. Especially Mack's, introducing her to his ex-wife.

Smiling and nodding in acknowledgment made her head ache.

Kimmy's welcoming hug tore the final rent in her heart.

Carly couldn't retreat fast enough. Murmuring something to Ray about aspirin and unpacking, she backed out of the house. The taxi driver had left her suitcase on the porch, and she ran with it down the walk, blinking against the pain.

She was well aware she didn't say goodbye.

Hadn't she had enough of those?

If Mack thought curses would help anything, he'd let loose with the mile-long string on the tip of his tongue. Gas pedal to the floor, he rushed over to Carly's.

She hadn't answered her phone this afternoon.

He hadn't wanted to leave the house until Suzanne had completed her visit and Kimmy was snuggled into bed.

Not that Suzanne was any kind of physical threat to their child, but sometimes one of her sporadic visits would give Kimmy a bedtime crying jag. Even though she'd gone to sleep easily, he'd keep an ear open for a 2:00 a.m. nightmare.

He tried pulling a breathful of oxygen into his lungs. His chest hurt from the weight of all his responsibilities dropping on him at once. He'd politely handled a surprise visit from his ex, fielded a call from John in Germany, tucked his daughter into bed after three stories and a glass of water.

Now he craved seeing Carly like he craved sleep. Desperately. To lighten his heart and mind.

But she hadn't answered her phone this afternoon. And some new sense he'd developed regarding her told him that was bad news. A curse-worthy situation.

He pulled into the parking lot of her condo and forced down another deep breath. He'd somehow make whatever was wrong right.

Two doorbell rings brought him nothing. A *rap-rap-rap* nothing more. He pounded in frustration with his fist.

And she thankfully, beautifully, opened the door. She wore another pair of men's boxers. A long T-shirt already sliding off one bare shoulder. Her curls were more fuzzy than frothy, and a pillowcase crease lined her cheek.

He smiled, burdens already lightening. "You look great."

"What do you want?" she asked.

"I'm sorry to wake you up, honey." He tried opening the screen door, found it locked.

"S'okay." She frowned. "What do you want, though?"

"Open up." He waggled his eyebrows. "I'll make it worth your while."

She shook her head. "Nuh-uh."

That weight resettled over his chest. Warning bells clanged in his ears. He had to yell to hear himself over them. "What do you mean, 'nuh-uh'?"

She blinked at his noise. "I mean you're not coming in."

The curses leaped out. "Damn, Carly, what the hell are you talking about? Please don't play with me right now, okay? I've had a hell of an afternoon and evening."

The porch light of the condo next door blinked on. Mack rattled the door impatiently.

"For goodness' sake." Rolling her eyes, Carly unlocked the screen and pushed it open.

Mack stepped inside and slammed the front door shut behind him. He wasn't so stupid as to try to touch her. Grabbing another lungful of air, he crossed his arms over his chest. "What's the matter? And don't try telling me 'nothing.'"

She crossed her own arms over her chest and was silent.

He took in the packed boxes scattered about the room. Pictures were off the walls. There was even a piece of packing tape stuck to the shirt she'd been sleeping in.

He stared at her. "Did you come home and do more packing?"

She frowned. A sense of betrayal burned through his gut, and he reached out to rip the length of tape off her shirt. "You did, didn't you? We spent the most spectacular night of *my* life together and you came home and continued packing."

Her gaze wouldn't meet his.

He rolled the tape into a ball and threw it across the room. "*Damn* you, Carly."

Her head lifted and her gray-green eyes pinned him. "Well, damn you right back. You think it was easy for me to arrive at your house after the most spectacular night of *my* life to find your ex-wife ensconced in your living room?"

He shook his head. "You can't be jealous of Suzanne. You can't believe she jeopardizes what we've found."

She waved a hand. "It's not about Suzanne. It's about *me*. What I want for my life."

Maybe they were getting somewhere. "And what's that, Carly? Tell me exactly what that is."

She closed her eyes and ran her fingers through her hair. The curls zigged and zagged, as obviously agitated as her mood. "I tried being with another man with an ex-wife and child. With all that baggage that comes along with it. I was hurt. Badly."

He knew how much his situation mirrored Peter's.

How Carly was afraid she'd fall in love with his daughter, his dad and his pets, then lose all of them if their relationship dissolved. He delved deeply for patience. "So given that, what is it you want now, Carly?"

"I want to be the love in a man's heart," she said hoarsely. "Not the second wife or the next woman in a man's life."

His heart pounded loudly in his ears, sounding like a whole team of size fifteen basketball shoes running across the gym floor. Heat speared his gut again. "So how do I fit in with that, huh?"

Her gaze dropped to her feet. "You don't, Mack. You and Kimmy and Ray and Grits and Cookies and Milk and Corndog and that snake. None of you fit with that."

More belly heat. Then a laugh as sharp and jagged as broken window glass came out of his mouth. Could he pick 'em, or what? "This is perfect. Absolutely perfect."

She shot him a wary glance.

"Don't worry about a thing, babe. I know exactly how to play this scene." The laugh erupted from him again, nearly piercing his chest on its way out. "You didn't think it would be this much trouble. So much clutter. So much *baggage*. We're bringing you down, holding you back."

Carly swallowed, opened her mouth.

He held up a hand. "No need to say anything. I've heard it before, and I should have seen it coming the first day we met. Hell, I *did* see it coming. Damn, but you're all alike. You leave when the going gets complicated."

And before another of his own laughs could wound him, he swung toward the door. "Just one thing." He didn't turn back to look at her.

"What?"

The words came out of his mouth without his permission. "How could you do it? How could you decide to not be with me and then settle in for a nice long nap?" He doubted that he'd ever sleep again.

"Because I wanted to forget," she said, her voice hoarse and faint. "It seemed the easiest way."

"How's my minister?" Carly asked her mother gaily, by way of greeting.

A weird little silence came over the phone.

"Mom? Mother? You okay?"

"Fine, dear. How are you? How was your business trip?"

"Rousing success. We got Cycle the contract with Muscle Machines." *And I got a broken heart.* What she'd felt for Peter had been the merest scratch compared to this.

"How is your packing coming?"

Carly went for cheerful again. "Almost all done." And a baptism of tears for every box.

"You don't sound yourself, Carly. What's wrong?"

Carly cleared her throat. "Just tired, Mom." Since Mack had left three days ago she hadn't slept. Not only had he jinxed her heart, he'd jinxed her ability to rest.

"When you get home we'll fix that. Comfort food and your old room."

Carly didn't want to tell her mother that she didn't think tuna noodle casserole and her old bedspread were going to heal her. But she smiled, anyway. "Hey, and I can be the true test of my minister's ability. If his sermons can keep *me* awake..."

Her mother's laughter sounded forced. "Carly, I want to tell you—"

The call-waiting click interrupted. "Oops, another call." How much she dreaded it was Mack. How much she hoped it was Mack. "I'll phone you later."

Carly clicked in the second call. "Hello?"

"Carly?" A young girl's voice.

Carly's heart jerked. *Kimmy?* "Yes?"

The voice came again, stronger, older than Kimmy's. "Carly, it's me, Laurel."

Tears burst at the corners of Carly's eyes. *"Laurel."* For the first time in days she really smiled.

They chatted for several minutes. Laurel thanked her for the birthday gift of the *Little House* books. She'd already read the first one. Carly told her that the last in the set, *These Happy Golden Years,* was her favorite, the one in which Laura Ingalls married her love. The little girl promised to call when she'd finished it.

"Only if it's okay with your mom, Laurel."

"She's right here," Laurel replied, "and wants to talk to you."

Carly's palms went sweaty as she waited to hear the other woman's voice. Maybe she was offended that Carly had sent the birthday gift. Maybe she'd tell her to keep out of Laurel's life.

But instead, Laurel's mother graciously seconded the thanks for the present.

Carly swallowed. "I'm so glad to hear that. I've always felt a special bond with Laurel, and I hoped the gift wouldn't be an intrusion.''

''Your love for Laurel is one of the good things I can think of that came out of Peter's and my divorce,'' the other woman said, then chuckled. ''Besides our remarriage.''

Carly laughed, too. ''Then I'm glad for all of us. And I'm glad Laurel and I can still be friends.''

''I would never want my daughter to turn away from love.''

Carly ended the call and sat down on one of the taped-up boxes, eased somewhat by her conversation with Laurel. It was good to think about her and smile again. A few months ago, because of the pain of losing her, Carly had been loath to let another child into her heart. But Kimmy had found her way there, and maybe someday she'd be able to smile thinking about her, too.

She rubbed at the spot between her breasts. ''Funny how much room a heart has,'' she said aloud. ''For Laurel and Kimmy and...''

Funny how much room a heart has. ''No.'' She said it aloud again, as if that would sever the mental connection. ''No.''

The words didn't work. Carly's stomach slid out of its normal spot to head for her suddenly wobbly knees. Hadn't she been afraid of throwing her cards in with Mack because of what she thought was the limited room in a human heart? She'd wanted to be the first wife because she hadn't believed there was room for any others.

And she herself had found plenty of space for Laurel

and Kimmy and Ray and Corndog and Grits and Cookies and Milk and...Mack.

Always Mack. Forever Mack.

But he'd never said he'd loved her. To be with him,
she *had* to be his love.

Mack had managed to stoke a good angry fire for
about three days. Every time he'd think of Carly, he'd
add another piece of kindling. Moving to Indiana. The
minister. Like Suzanne did before her, leaving when
the going got tough.

After a couple of days, though, he was down to her
skittishness about mice and her laughter over his own
dislike of snakes. That's when he decided to just go
ahead and let the misery douse the flames.

Mack realized he didn't do *miserable* well. Instead
of being a wallower, he was a doer, a doer always
looking for solutions. He kept running his last conversation with Carly over in his mind.

She'd claimed that Kimmy, his father, the pets,
didn't fit in with what she wanted for her life. Easy.
That was just so much dog, uh, *droppings* like he shov-
eled off the back grass every day. A woman who
played card games, danced and tied ribbons like she
did wanted all of them. She'd just been afraid to attach
to Kimmy *et al.* in case she lost them like she lost that
other little girl, Laurel.

No, the problem wasn't Kimmy, Dad or the animals.
The problem was *him.*

She didn't want to be the second wife or the next
woman in a man's life.

Hell. That was the sticker. He couldn't erase the

past—wouldn't even want to, since it had brought him his daughter.

And then, finally, he remembered something else, like it had been hovering around him for days, waiting for just this moment to kick him in the butt.

He'd asked her what she wanted, and until this moment he'd forgotten the very first thing she'd said.

"I want to be the love in a man's heart."

Was she the love in his?

Nobody was more distrustful of the emotion than him. Marrying Suzanne had been another burden, really. Another task. Someone else to make happy.

He'd failed at it. Making him a cynical, bitter, nonbeliever in love. He'd avoided the responsibility of a relationship since then.

But would a relationship truly be such a burden?

Not with Carly.

He remembered how well they tackled Cycle Software projects. How she'd shared the tedious burden of number crunching in San Francisco. How he'd relaxed as she talked his daughter to sleep.

He remembered how she'd made love to him, and when he was still stunned by the passion, she'd asked, "Doesn't anybody ever make it easier for you?"

Carly did.

Of the people in his life, it was she who reminded him he was a man, it was she who lightened his load.

It was she who renewed his ability to love.

Carly recognized the pattern. The doorbell, followed by a demanding *rat-a-tat-tat*, followed by an impatient rattle of the screen door handle.

Her palms immediately began to sweat. She wiped them on her shorts, and then, heart squealing in agony, she pulled open the door to let Mack in. No use putting off the pain.

He blinked in the sudden dimness of her nearly bare living room. She blinked, too, because in one hand he held a plastic bag of water and in the other, a cassette tape.

"Hi," he said grimly.

Four days hadn't changed anything. Her stomach flip-flopped, her heart shredded, and heat burst over the back of her neck. "You look tired," she said, then immediately wished the words back.

His gaze ran over her, focused in on her face. "You, too," he said softly.

A nervous babble erupted from her mouth. "I've checked out with Lisa. My last paycheck will be cut Friday. I handed in my keys to the old building. I've been in contact with John, and he's confident you'll do fine without me—"

"John doesn't know what he's talking about."

Carly swallowed. "Huh? No. Seriously. John told me you don't need me."

"And I told you John doesn't know what he's talking about."

Another blast of heat scorched her nape. She twisted her fingers together in front of her, not sure what he was getting at.

He turned his head to look about the bare room. "Your bedroom like this, too?"

Frowning, she nodded. Her gaze snagged again on that water-filled bag. Were those fish swimming around? He must have bought some new pets for Kimmy and been unwilling to leave them in the car.

"Where's your stereo?" he asked abruptly.

"Packed away."

Her answer appeared to pain him. "What about your bedroom? I remember seeing a tape deck, clock radio combo."

Blocking off the memory of him in her bedroom, she held up her wrist. "I'm using the alarm on my watch these days. I packed up the clock radio, too."

He looked almost queasy.

"Are you all right?" she asked.

"That depends."

The answer alarmed her. Two steps forward and she was able to lay her palm against his forehead. For comparison, she put her other one against her own. They both seemed the same temperature.

Carly glanced at his face, then jumped. He was smiling at her, a sweet, blazing smile that could almost heal a heart.

"You're taking care of me again," he said.

"Why are you here?" she whispered.

He held up the tape. "I came to play you a song. I thought it would make you understand."

"'Summer Sounds of the Past,'" she read off the spine of the tape. "Make me understand what?"

"Damn. I wanted to play the song." He shuffled his feet. "Maybe if I sang a line or two you'd remember it."

Carly's heart started to stutter, and the flush of heat on her neck ran over her entire body. "Why this song?"

He looked into her eyes and his were deep-dark and serious and she had to fight to keep herself from touching him again. "This is my 'first love' song. I was fourteen years old, and it was summer and this song was playing when I discovered what love felt like."

He swallowed and his voice went a note hoarser. "The sun was hot on my shoulders and hot on my hair and I knew why Shakespeare had written *Romeo and Juliet* and why people got married and why my uncle Jasper had cried at the grave of my aunt June."

Tears pricked Carly's eyes, and she blinked them away. "So who was this girl, this first love?"

He shook his head. "I don't remember her name." He paused, taking a long, deep breath. "I just remember how I felt that day and how I never felt it again until I met you."

Carly reached for the wall to steady her. *"What?"* she said. "What are you saying?"

Instead of answering, he started singing. Just a couple of lines. More tears sprang to her eyes. He halted, red tingeing his cheeks. "Do you recognize it?" he asked.

Obviously Mack couldn't carry a tune in a Hefty bag. She had no idea what song he'd been singing. But she nodded, still afraid to let go of the wall.

"I'm trying to tell you that I love you, Carly," he said. "You may not have been the one in my heart when the song first played, but you're the one in my heart now, and you're one that will make my life easier, better. You're the only one I know will be there forever."

"Oh." Maybe the earth was moving again, maybe

it was an earthquake this time, because the wall wasn't stable enough, and she had to hold on to Mack to keep upright. His heart beat wildly against her ear.

"What do you say?" he whispered against her temple.

"I—" There was such potential for heartbreak in his arms. People and animals to love, to lose.

As if he sensed her fears, he dangled the plastic bag in front of her eyes. Three fish, neon bright in red and blue, swam about. "I brought you something else. These guys are just a symbol, you know. To show my trust that you can care for us forever, just like we want to care for you."

The fish were blue like wide-open sky and red like the pumping blood in her miraculously healed heart. "Oh, God, Mack. I love you," she said, and the words hurt so good—just like a love song sung sincerely, but pathetically out of tune.

Beep.

"Carly. Oh, you're not there." Through the answering machine, Carly's mother's voice hovered somewhere between tearful and ecstatic. "I really need to tell you this right away."

A happy hiccup came through clearly. "I've already had one glass of champagne, and Matthew, Minister Hawkins, *Matthew,* well, he said I should call you right away."

She giggled. "But I said that already, didn't I? Well, dear, I hope you won't be too disappointed. I hope you won't be hurt. We always said it was just our little joke, you marrying the minister. But—well—" Another hiccup followed by a giggle. ''Well, the minister *is* getting married…to me!''

In the bedroom, under the fussy, romantic coverlets, two people stopped moving against one another at the end of the startling announcement.

Carly stared wide-eyed at the man who'd just asked *her* to become his wife. ''My mother's getting married. I don't know whether to laugh or to cry.''

Mack touched her cheek and instantly resolved to start his freckle count at the very earliest opportunity. But then a deeper resolve struck him, and he traced her mouth with shaking fingertips. How he loved her. How he'd make her happy. How they would share their burdens and their lives. ''Oh, honey, over the next fifty years we're going to find plenty of opportunity to do both.''

* * * * *

Available September 1998
from Silhouette Books...

World's Most
Eligible Bachelors

THE CATCH
OF CONARD COUNTY
by Rachel Lee

Rancher Jeff Cumberland: long, lean, sexy as sin. He's eluded every marriage-minded female in the county. Until a mysterious woman breezes into town and brings her fierce passion to his bed. Will this steamy Conard County courtship take September's hottest bachelor off of the singles market?

Each month, Silhouette Books brings you an irresistible bachelor in these all-new, original stories. Find out how the sexiest, most sought-after men are finally caught...

Available at your favorite retail outlet.

Silhouette ®

Take 2 bestselling love stories FREE

Plus get a FREE surprise gift!

Special Limited-Time Offer

Mail to Silhouette Reader Service™

3010 Walden Avenue
P.O. Box 1867
Buffalo, N.Y. 14269-1867

YES! Please send me 2 free Silhouette Yours Truly™ novels and my free surprise gift. Then send me 4 brand-new novels every other month, which I will receive months before they appear in bookstores. Bill me at the low price of $2.90 each plus 25¢ delivery and applicable sales tax, if any.* That's the complete price, and a saving of over 10% off the cover prices—quite a bargain! I understand that accepting the books and gift places me under no obligation ever to buy any books. I can always return a shipment and cancel at any time. Even if I never buy another book from Silhouette, the 2 free books and the surprise gift are mine to keep forever.

201 SEN CH72

Name	(PLEASE PRINT)	
Address	Apt. No.	
City	State	Zip

This offer is limited to one order per household and not valid to present Silhouette Yours Truly™ subscribers. *Terms and prices are subject to change without notice. Sales tax applicable in N.Y.

USYT-98 ©1996 Harlequin Enterprises Limited

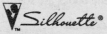

International bestselling author

JOAN JOHNSTON

continues her wildly popular Hawk's Way
miniseries with an all-new, longer-length novel

THE SUBSTITUTE GROOM
HAWK'S WAY

August 1998

Jennifer Wright's hopes and dreams had rested on her summer wedding—until a single moment changed everything.
Including the *groom*. Suddenly Jennifer agreed to marry her
fiancé's best friend, a darkly handsome Texan she needed—
and desperately wanted—almost against her will. But U.S.
Air Force Major Colt Whitelaw had sacrificed too much to
settle for a marriage of convenience, and that made hiding
her passion all the more difficult. And hiding her biggest
secret downright impossible…

**"Joan Johnston does contemporary Westerns
to perfection."** —*Publishers Weekly*

Available in August 1998
wherever Silhouette books are sold.

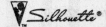

Coming September 1998

Three delightful stories about the blessings
and surprises of "Labor" Day.

TABLOID BABY by Candace Camp

She was whisked to the hospital in the nick of time....

THE NINE-MONTH KNIGHT
by Cait London

A down-on-her-luck secretary is experiencing
odd little midnight cravings....

THE PATERNITY TEST by Sherryl Woods

The stick turned blue before her
biological clock struck twelve....

*These three special women are very pregnant...and very
single, although they won't be either for too much longer,
because baby—and Daddy—are on their way!*

Available at your favorite retail outlet.